Simon Somerville Laurie

John Amos Comenius - Bishop of the Moravians

his life and educational works

Simon Somerville Laurie

John Amos Comenius - Bishop of the Moravians
his life and educational works

ISBN/EAN: 9783337400644

Printed in Europe, USA, Canada, Australia, Japan

Cover: Foto ©Andreas Hilbeck / pixelio.de

More available books at **www.hansebooks.com**

(𝔓𝔦𝔱𝔱 𝔓𝔯𝔢𝔰𝔰 𝔖𝔢𝔯𝔦𝔢𝔰.)

JOHN AMOS COMENIUS

BISHOP OF THE MORAVIANS

HIS LIFE AND EDUCATIONAL WORKS

BY

S. S. LAURIE, A.M., F.R.S.E.

PROFESSOR OF THE INSTITUTES AND HISTORY OF EDUCATION
IN THE UNIVERSITY OF EDINBURGH;

AUTHOR OF 'PRIMARY INSTRUCTION IN RELATION TO
EDUCATION,' 'PHILOSOPHY OF ETHICS,' ETC.

THIRD EDITION, REVISED.

CAMBRIDGE:

AT THE UNIVERSITY PRESS.

1887

PREFACE TO SECOND EDITION.

In issuing the second edition of this book it occurs to me to say that it is possible that a critical mind examining *any one* of Comenius's writings might here and there take exception to my statement of his opinions. It is therefore necessary to explain that wherever the opinions expressed by Comenius in any of his Treatises was subsequently modified, I have given his final views.

For the rest, I can only repeat what I stated in the preface to the first edition, that this book is the most complete—so far as I know the only complete—account of Comenius and his works that exists in any language. I have gone carefully through the four volumes of his didactic writings, containing 2271 pages of Latin, good, bad, and indifferent. The German translation of one of the treatises has also been before me. The life is written, like the rest of the book, entirely from a collation of original sources; but I do not endeavour to give an account of Comenius's *ecclesiastical* relations.

It is not always easy to determine how much of a voluminous and prolix writer should be given. My object has been to omit nothing essential. There is much in Comenius that is fanciful, and even fantastic, and of this I have endeavoured, in suitable places, to give enough to exhibit the author's manner of thought. There is much, again, that is now universally accepted in education, which I have yet preserved, because the statement of it is essential to a proper exposition of Comenius's system. My aim has been to omit nothing that is characteristic or useful, or historically important.

The scholastic habit of division and subdivision was inherited by Comenius, and along with this he had in great force the systematising impulse of the German mind, though not himself a German. He can leave nothing to be understood, but will sometimes imperil his whole theory by insisting on the small as well as the great. While following closely the argument of Comenius I have dropped superfluous divisions and distinctions, but wholly to avoid repetition was impracticable.[1]

S. S. LAURIE.

University of Edinburgh.
March, 1884.

[1] A pleasing and lucid sketch of Comenius and his work will be found in Quick's *Educational Biographies.*

CONTENTS.

INTRODUCTION.

THE REVIVAL OF LETTERS.

IT is usual to date the revival of letters from the time of Petrarch in Italy (1304-74) and Chaucer in England (1328-1400), and to find the chief impulse which the movement received from without, in the dispersal of Greek scholars over Europe at the taking of Constantinople by the Turks in 1453. The new birth of the mind of Western and Northern Europe was a process similar to that which is repeated in the intellectual history of every man who questions and throws aside the conventionalities of life and opinion in the midst of which he has grown up. The mind of Europe was oppressed with a burden of pedantry of form and dogmatism in theology, ritual, philosophy, grammar, and rhetoric. Looking straight at things—things of sense and of thought, contemplating those questions which every thoughtful man has ultimately to answer for himself, in a direct way and no longer through the medium of mere phrases and formulae, constituted the essence of the revival. The regeneration of the human spirit was felt in almost every department of intellectual and moral activity. It is a mistake however to think

A

that there was any sudden breach of the continuity of European life in the Revival. There had been an awakening on the subject of education in the time of Charlemagne and the University movement of the twelfth century had familiarised men's minds with the re-discussion of old problems. Ancient Greek learning had also for some time been influencing the leaders of thought through the Latin translations from the Arabic.

This return of the soul of man to Reality—the attempt to penetrate to the truth of things through the hardened crust of verbalism and dogma was, it seems to me, the true characteristic of the revival. For the dry bones of Grammar, Logic, and Rhetoric, was now substituted the living substance of thought, and the intellectual gymnastic of the schools gave place to the free play of mind once more striving to bring itself into contact with nature. The revival was thus a return to realism—the realism, that is to say, of the thought of man exercised directly on the things that pertain to humanity.

The classical writers of Greece and Rome were, in those days, almost the sole exponents of the new life. and the alliance in them of truth and felicity of perception with beauty of expression so captivated the minds of the learned men of all civilized countries that they surrendered to them their own individuality. Beauty of expression was regarded as inseparable from truth and elevation of thought. The former was held to be the guarantee of the latter. The movement soon shared the fate of all enthusiasms. The new form was worshipped as the old had been, and to it the spirit and substance were subordinated. Style became the supreme object of the educated class, and successful imitation, and thereafter laborious criticism, became the marks of the highest culture. The relation of ancient Rome to Greece was somewhat similar, but with this difference, that the Roman, being himself cast in an antique mould, brought into literature the contribution of his own vigour and originality.

When style and a wide and various knowledge of stylists became the ambition of the cultivated man, it can readily be understood that the education of boys suffered. The object of schoolmasters being to prepare boys to admire and imitate perfection of form in an ancient tongue, they had for this purpose to fall back on the old grammatical drill. The chief permanent benefit to youth was an improvement in the text-books, the works of the classical writers themselves now taking the place of epitomes of Logic and Rhetoric baldly expressed in barbarous Latinity.

It would have been strange if, in this spring time, man's relations to the unseen and eternal had escaped the criticism of the reawakened soul: accordingly, we find the names of Wycliffe and Huss conspicuous in the period of Petrarch and Chaucer. When, later, subjects of spiritual interest came fully within the scope of the modern movement, they took precedence of all others, for they concerned the business and touched the heart of the humblest as well as of the highest. Reform in religion introduced the element of passion into the revival, and supplied the motive force necessary to sustained and persistent activity. This introduction of the element of religious passion marks what may be called the second revival at the end of the fifteenth century.

In the earlier half of the sixteenth century the Classical or Humanistic movement was represented by such men as Ludovicus Vives, Erasmus, Budæus, and Sir Thomas More, and the parallel religious activity by the great names of Luther and Calvin. In Melanchthon the literary and theological streams met. Luther was unquestionably a Humanist, but it was inevitable that the deeper spiritual interests of which he was the guardian should obscure the less urgent and less vital claims of learning and culture. In his followers this result was conspicuous. Men's minds became engrossed with a reconstruction of faith and a reorganisation of the Church, an enterprise which shook Europe and disturbed the old order to its foundations. The political and ecclesiastical wars may be said to have lasted nearly one hundred and thirty years.

In the History of Education it is important to recognise the existence of the two parallel streams of intellectual and spiritual regeneration. The leaders of both, like the leaders of all great social changes, at once bethought themselves of the schools. Their hope was in the young, and hence the reform of Education early engaged their attention.

The pure Humanists, on the one hand, were intent on the substitution of literary culture for grammatical and logical forms, and cared only for the education of the few; but their sympathy with the religious reformation was notorious and they shared the suspicion with which the Protestant Reformers were regarded by the mediæval Church. To know Greek was to be exposed to insinuations of heresy. An attitude of hostility towards the independent activity of the human mind was not, however, peculiar to the mediæval Church; it is to be easily detected in certain forms of Protestantism. Both alike are obscurantist, and regard Reason with suspicion, if not with aversion. They have a profound distrust of Humanity.

The Church Reformers, on the other hand, had an interest in the progress of culture scarcely less sincere than that of the Humanists, but to this they added compassion for the dense ignorance of the masses of the people. The human soul, wherever found, was to them an object of infinite concern, and, unlike the Humanists, they aimed at universal instruction. The new form of the old faith, it was felt, could sustain itself only on the basis of popular education. The Reformers were educational philanthropists in the truest sense, and hence the people's school is rightly called the child of the Reformation. It would be out of place here, in illustration of what has been said, to do more than advert to Luther's impassioned appeals, and to Melanchthon's universal activity which earned for him the honourable designation of Præceptor Germaniæ. To the same union of the theological with the philanthropic spirit was due the noble scheme of popular education embodied in the Book of Polity of the Reformed Church of Scotland, written so early as 1560.

The educational aims of the leaders of the Humanistic and Theological revival respectively, while they did not conflict, were thus different both in their spirit and scope; and it is important to note this, if we are to understand the history of Schools from the sixteenth century down to our own time: for motive causes in operation 350 years ago are still active.

While the literary Humanists, such as Erasmus, had for their aim culture, and this almost exclusively through the literatures of Greece and Rome, the theological Humanists, though recognising culture, yet desired to subordinate it at every stage to a religious purpose. The latter had consequently on their side popular sentiment, because they most truly represented the popular need. 'Above all things,' said Luther, 'let the Scriptures be the chief and the most frequently used reading-book, both in primary and in *high* schools. . . . Where the Holy Scriptures do not bear sway, there I would counsel none to send his child; for every institution will degenerate where God's Word is not in daily exercise. . . . The High Schools ought to send forth men thoroughly versed in the Scriptures to become bishops and pastors, and to stand in the van against heretics, the devil, and, if need be, the whole world.' With all this, Luther's views of education were large and liberal, including music, gymnastic, and history, as well as the languages and mathematics. Melanchthon also, while urging the pursuit of ancient philosophy in its original sources, and of the literatures of Greece and Rome, yet held by Christian teaching as the main

end of the school. So with Valentine Trotzendorf.
The distinguished friend of Luther and of the English
Ascham, John Sturm of Strasburg, whose great classical
school was a model for all countries, propounded as his
educational aim 'a wise and persuasive piety, knowledge,
and purity and elegance of diction.' The Humanistic
Protestant schools thus embraced Christian teaching
as a vital part of their curriculum, the desire of the
Reformers being always to unite true learning with
sound theology. It was this theological humanism (so
to speak) that ultimately gained the day among the
Reformed Churches.

The Roman Catholic Church meanwhile was not
insensible to the scholastic changes which the modern
spirit had made inevitable. The new order of the
Jesuits was authorised in 1540. Their special function
as a Church Society was preaching, confession, and
education, but the last-named chiefly. 'To this,' says
Ranke, 'they thought of binding themselves by a special
clause in their vows; and although that was not done,
they made the practice of this duty imperative by the
most cogent rules. Their most earnest desire was to
gain the rising generation.' In 1626 they had already
467 Colleges and thirty-six Seminaries, and to their
zealous and self-denying labours the reaction from
Protestantism was mainly due. While subordinating
all learning, nay, every act of life, to the Catholic
idea, they yet had open minds for educational improvements. The best parts of the methods pursued in
the schools of Trotzendorf and Sturm were embodied

in their system.   Familiarity with Latin as a common
language, however, rather than with the literature of
Latin, was their school aim.   At the same time, they
were sufficiently influenced by the Humanistic revival
to discard scholastic barbarism and to cultivate style.
Where rhetoric and style are cultivated for themselves,
the result is a certain discipline of the faculties certainly,
but an absence of the genuine substance of education.
There could be no danger to the Church in this; for,
with such aims, expression, not thought, becomes the
prime consideration; and it is only thought about the
realities of sense or about the products of thought itself
that calls forth original power.   The Jesuit course included Latin and a moderate amount of Greek, with
logic and rhetoric for the more advanced classes.   They
could show as good a curriculum as the public grammar
schools of their time, and a much better organisation.
The superiority of the Protestant schools lay in the
greater freedom of spirit which characterised them, and
the greater regard paid to the substance of literature.
The Jesuits, however, were far in advance of their con-
temporaries in laying down for their teachers a definite
educational method—stiff and inelastic certainly, but yet
a method.   Little by little, little at a time, cultivation of
the memory, thoroughness in a few things, easy and
graduated work, and a mild but persistent discipline, were
merits belonging to the Jesuit schools two hundred
years before they were practised to any large extent
elsewhere.   It is not our business here to enter more
largely into the Jesuit system: our object is simply to

show that this religious Order accepted the Humanistic movement, under narrow restrictions certainly, but these not of a kind to render their Humanism a mere name.

Thus it was that on both sides of the great controversy which began 350 years ago, and still continues, religion furnished the prime motive of education; and so it will ever be, although it is possible that the form which the religious spirit takes may be so veiled as to be invisible even to itself. On one side, it was recognised that the way to faith was through obedience, and that obedience, the first of virtues in a true Catholic, can be secured in two ways—by the careful shaping of the minds of those who demand education, and by the equally careful neglect of the intelligence of those who can be safely passed by. On the other side, the Humanistic revival was early lost in the more pressing claims of the Theological revival, and the genuine humane spirit permanently survived only in the movement to instruct the masses. The theological spirit it was that gave the impulse necessary to carry education down into the lower strata of society, and so to raise the humanity of the people. In the presence of the competing claims of the two Theologies pure Humanism could not sustain itself.

Accordingly the scholastic improvements effected under the influence of Melanchthon and Sturm[1], and, in England, of Colet, Lillie and Ascham, did not endure, save in a very limited sense. Pure classical literature was now read,—a great gain certainly, but this was all. There was no tradition of method, as was the case

[1] Sturm died at the age of 83 in 1589.

in the Jesuit order. During the latter half of the sixteenth century, the complaints made of the state of the schools, the waste of time, the barbarous and intricate grammar rules, the cruel discipline, were loud and long, and proceeded from men of the highest intellectual standing. It has to be remembered, however, that all Europe had been embroiled in civil and ecclesiastical contentions, and that the seeds of popular education and of an improved secondary system could not possibly have developed themselves in an atmosphere so ungenial. Indeed, until the remodelled school code of Saxony appeared in 1773 the dawn so full of promise was clouded. Two hundred years were lost. Scotland alone was during this period busily carrying out, in a truly national sense, the programme of the Reformation and the Humanists, but this, in accordance with the genius of Protestantism, mainly on the popular side.

But the complaints and demands of men of learning and piety were not relaxed. To unity in the Reformed Churches they looked, but looked in vain, for a settlement of opinion, and to the school they looked as the sole hope of the future. The school, as it actually existed, might have well filled them with despair. Even in the Universities, Aristotelian Physics and Metaphysics, and with them the scholastic philosophy, still held their own. The reforms initiated mainly by Melanchthon had not, indeed, contemplated the overthrow of Aristotelianism. He and the other Humanists merely desired to substitute Aristotle himself in the original for the Latin translation from the Arabic (necessarily misleading), and the Greek and Latin classics for barbarous epitomes. These very reforms, however, perpetuated the reign of Aristotle, when the spirit that actuated the Reformers was dead and there had been a relapse into the old scholasticism. The Jesuit reaction, also, which recovered France and South Germany for the Papal See, was powerful enough to preserve a footing for the metaphysical theology of St Thomas Aquinas and the schoolmen. In England, Milton was of opinion that the youth of the Universities were, even so late as his time, still presented with an 'asinine feast of sow-thistles.' These retrogressions in School and University serve to show how exceedingly difficult it is to contrive any system of education, middle or upper, which will work of itself when the contrivers pass from the scene. Hence the importance, it seems to us, of having in every University, as part of the philosophical faculty, a department for the exposition of this very question of Education—surely a very important subject in itself as an academic study, and in its practical relations transcending perhaps all others. How are the best traditions of educational theory and practice to be preserved and handed down, if those who are to instruct the youth of the country are to be sent forth to their work from our Universities with minds absolutely vacant as to the principles and history of their profession—if they have never been taught to ask themselves the questions, 'What am I going to do?' 'Why?' and 'How?' This subject is one worthy of consideration both by the Universities and the State. It was the want of Method that led to the decline of Schools after the Reformation period; it was the study of Method which gave the Jesuits the superiority that on many parts of the Continent they still retain.

In 1605 there appeared a book which was destined to place educational method on a scientific foundation, although its mission is not yet, it is true, accomplished. This was Francis Bacon's *Advancement of Learning*, which was followed, some years later, by the *Organon*. For some time the thoughts of men had been turning to the study of Nature. Bacon represented this movement, and gave it the necessary impulse by his masterly survey of the domain of human knowledge, his pregnant suggestions, and his formulation of scientific method. Bacon was not aware of his relations to the science and art of Education; he praises the Jesuit schools, not knowing that he was by his philosophy subverting their very foundations. We know inductively: that was the sum of Bacon's teaching. In the sphere of outer Nature, the scholastic saying, *Nihil est in intellectu quod non prius fuerit in sensu*, was accepted, but with this addition, that the impressions on our senses were not themselves to be trusted. The mode of verifying sense-impressions, and the grounds of valid and necessary inference, had to be investigated and applied. It is manifest that if we can tell *how* it is we *know*, it follows that the method of intellectual instruction is scientifically settled.

But Bacon not only represented the urgent longing for a co-ordination of the sciences and for a new method, he also represented the weariness of words, phrases, and vain subtleties which had been gradually growing in strength since the time of Rabelais, Montaigne, Ludovicus Vives, and Erasmus. The poets, also, had been placing Nature before the minds of men in a new aspect. The Humanists, as we have said, while unquestionably improving the aims and procedure of education, had been powerless to prevent the tendency to fall once more under the dominion of words, and to revert to mere form. The realism of human life and thought, which constituted their *raison d'être*, had been unable to sustain itself as a principle of action, because there was no school of method. It was the study of the realities of sense that was finally to place education on a scientific basis, and make reaction, as to method at least, impossible.

The thought of any age determines the education of the age which is to succeed it. Education follows, it does not lead. The School and the Church alike march in the wake of science, philosophy, and political ideas. We see this illustrated in every epoch of human history, and in none so conspicuously as in the changes which occurred in the philosophy and education of ancient Rome during the lifetime of the elder Cato, and, in modern times, during the revival of letters and the subsequent rise of the Baconian induction. It is impossible, indeed, for any great movement of thought to find acceptance without its telling to some extent on every department of the body politic. Its influence on the ideas entertained as to the education

of the rising generation must be, above all, distinct
and emphatic. Every philosophical writer on political
science has recognised this, and has felt the vast significance of the educational system of a country both as
an effect—the consequence of a revolution in thought—
and as a cause, a moving force of incalculable power in
the future life of a commonwealth. Thus it was that
the Humanistic movement which preceded and accompanied the Reformation of religion shook to its
centre the mediæval school-system of Europe; and
that subsequently the silent rise of the inductive spirit
subverted its foundations.

Bacon, though not himself a Realist in the modern
and abused sense of that term, was the father of Realism.
It was this side of his teaching which was greedily seized
upon, and even exaggerated. Educational zeal now ran
in this channel. The conviction of the Churches of the
time, that one can make men what one pleases (by fair
means or foul), was shared by the innovators. By
education, rightly conceived and rightly applied, the
enthusiasts dreamed that they could manufacture men,
and, in truth, the Jesuits had shown that a good deal
could be done in this direction. The new enthusiasts
failed to see that the genius of Protestantism is the
genius of freedom, and that man refuses to be manufactured except on suicidal terms. He must first
sacrifice that which is his distinctive title to manhood
—his personality. That the prophets of educational
Realism should have failed to see this is not to be laid at
their door as a fault: it merely shows that they belonged

to their own time and not to ours. They failed then, as some fail now, to understand man and his education, because they break with the past. The record of the past is with them as it was with the Baconian realists, merely a record of blunders. The modern Humanist more wisely accepts it as the storehouse of the thoughts and life of human reason. In the life of Man each individual of the race best finds his own true life. This is modern Humanism—the Realism of thought.

Yet it is to the Sense-realists of the earlier half of the seventeenth century that we owe the scientific foundations of educational method, and the only indication of the true line of answer to the complaints of the time. In their hands sense-realism became allied with Protestant Theology, and pure Humanism disappeared. They were represented first by Wolfgang von Ratich (Ratke), a native of Holstein, born in 1571. Ratich was a man of considerable learning. The distractions of Europe, and the want of harmony, especially among the Churches of the Reformation, led him to consider how a remedy might be found for many existing evils. He thought that the remedy was to be found in an improved school-system—improved in respect both of the substance and method of teaching. In 1612, accordingly, he laid before the Diet of the German Empire at Frankfort a Memorial in which he promised, 'with the help of God, to give instruction for the service and welfare of all Christendom:' and to show—

'1. How the Hebrew, Greek, Latin, and other tongues

may easily be taught and learned both by young and old, more thoroughly and in a shorter time.

'2. How, not only in High Dutch, but also in other tongues, a school may be established in which the thorough knowledge of all Arts and Sciences may be learned and propagated.

'3. How, in the whole kingdom, one and the same speech, one and the same government, and, finally, one and the same religion, may be commodiously and peacefully maintained.'

We speak of Ratich here, not with a view to the exposition of his system, but merely as the pioneer of the modern inductive school, and as the predecessor of Comenius; and it will suffice, therefore, to sum up his leading principles as these are to be found stated by Schmidt and Von Raumer in their Histories :—

1. Everything according to the order and course of Nature[1].

2. Only one thing of a kind at a time[2].

3. One thing often repeated (*i.e.* keep at the same thing, repeating it often).

4. Everything in the mother-tongue first : for in the mother-tongue resides this advantage, that the pupil has to think only of the *thing* he has to learn, and need not

---

[1] The American translation should always be compared with the German; *e.g.* the German of Von Raumer is 'Alles nach Ordnung oder Lauff der Natur,' which is translated 'Everything in its order, or the course of Nature.' Schmidt says *und*, not *oder*.

[2] The American translation says 'Only one thing at a time,' and it equally misses the point elsewhere.

trouble himself with the language over and above. Out of the mother-tongue pass to other tongues.

5. Everything without violence. For by compulsion and blows one disgusts youth with studies, and causes them to assume an attitude of hostility to them. The pupil must not be afraid of the teacher, but love him, and hold him in honour, a result which will be found if the teacher rightly discharges his function. (Discipline was to be in the hands of a special functionary called the Scholarch.)

6. Nothing must be learned by rote, for intelligence and acuteness are absent from the pupil who gives himself much to rote-learning.

7. Uniformity in all things, as well in the method of teaching as in the books, rules, etc., so that the grammar of the various languages taught may be as much as possible harmonised.

8. First a thing in itself, and then the way of it. Matter before form. Rules without matter confuse the understanding.

9. Everything through experience and the investigation of particulars.

The motto of the Ratichians was '*Per inductionem et experimentum omnia*[1].'

Ratich's life was practically a failure. He did not succeed in his scholastic work, and this is to be ascribed to the following causes—(1) His character; (2) the too

---

[1] Raumer is a prejudiced writer, especially when dealing with Ratich and the 'moderns' (as he calls them) generally.

purely theoretical groundwork of his scheme; (3) the jealousy and opposition of others; (4) his wrong application of his own principles; (5) his want of that instinctive feeling for the *art* of teaching, which was conspicuous in his greater successor Comenius. He died in 1635, at the age of sixty-four. His scheme had meanwhile been most favourably received by many learned men, and had attracted the attention of the Princes of Central Europe. The University of Giessen reported favourably on his pretensions, and the Ratichians were by no means a small or uninfluential party in the schools and Universities of Europe. In those days some Universities seemed to take an interest in Education as a possible science.

The torch that fell from Ratich's hand was seized, ere it touched the ground, by John Amos Comenius, who became the head, and still continues the head, of the Sense-realistic school. His works have a present and practical, and not merely an historical and speculative, significance.

LIFE AND WORKS OF COMENIUS.

JOHN AMOS COMENIUS (Komenski) was born at Nivnitz, a village of Moravia,[1] on the 28th of March 1592. His father was a miller. The family belonged to the sect of Reformed Christians known sometimes as the Bohemian, more generally as the Moravian, Brethren. This sect of Christians has never attained to great dimensions, but it has been distinguished by an activity and zeal which have given it, notwithstanding the fewness of its members, a conspicuous place among religious communions. Although generally recognised as Lutherans, they connect themselves by direct ecclesiastical descent with the Bohemian Reformer Huss, and have always preserved a distinct organisation of their own. At the present day they number, it is believed, only about 5000 communicants in Europe, and 7000 in America. They acknowledge an episcopate, but their bishops have little power. Their chief characteristic seems always to have been a certain simplicity of faith, combined with an earnest personal

[1] Some say at *Comna* or *Comnia* (near Brünn), whence the surname Comnenius or Comenius.   The family name was in German *Töpfer, i.e.* Potter.   Comnia is in long. about 18° E. from Greenwich, lat. 49°.   Gindely simply says in the vicinity of *Ungarisch-Brod.*   At the University of Heidelberg he was entered as a native of Nivnitz, a little village about a league from Ungarisch-Brod.

piety and a practical realisation of the brotherly relation in which all the members of a common Christian
Confession ought to stand to one another.

Comenius is usually called an Austro-Sclav; that is
to say, a Sclav born within the sovereignty of Austria.
His family, and he himself consequently, spoke the
Bohemian or Czech tongue, which is a West-Sclav
dialect, and is considered to be the best of all the
Sclavonic forms. Huss may be said to have done for
this dialect what Luther afterwards did for German.

The young Comenius was born in troublous times.
The European disturbances and complications arising
out of the advance which the thought of man had
made in the fifteenth and sixteenth centuries—generally
denoted by the terms 'Revival of Letters' and the
'Reformation of Religion,' or more generally ' the
Renaissance,'—had already been in active operation for
seventy years, and Comenius was growing old when the
close of the Thirty Years' War gave Europe peace,
after having made a great part of it a desert. Austria
was at that time the great German power. Prussia had
no political existence, while Poland was a large and
influential kingdom, including much of what is now
Russia.

Comenius's parents died while he was still a child, and
he was accordingly handed over to guardians. There
appears to have been a little money left by the father—
enough to help in the education and maintenance of the
son. He received, however, only the limited amount
of instruction obtainable in one of those elementary

people's schools, which were the fruit of the Reformation—the school of Strassnick. This amounted to reading, writing, a knowledge of the Catechism, and of the
smallest beginnings of arithmetic. He had reached his
sixteenth year without having entered on the study of —
Latin—at that time still the indispensable instrument of
all literature, and of international communication among
the learned. We are not to conclude from this that his
guardians neglected his education. The community of
which he was an orphan child had to raise up pastors for
their own instruction, and this necessity, independently
of other considerations, would have led to the fostering
of any boyish promise shown by young Comenius.
It is probable that he was a child of slow growth. It
was certainly not till his sixteenth year that he began
to feel and to show a desire for the life of a scholar.
There was probably an advantage in this. Unvisited
by ambitions which could carry him beyond the narrow
limits of his own quiet community, his mind must have
had time slowly and surely to imbibe the teachings of
the simple Brotherhood to which he belonged, and to
be thoroughly imbued with their earnest spirit. We
see the effects of this upbringing conspicuous throughout his whole life. Simplicity, zeal, piety, self-sacrifice,
humility, are always present. The whole tenor of his
life confirms his own confession that he was by nature
of a retiring disposition, had more of fear than of hope
in his constitution, that the part of innovator was one
alien to him, and that he was keenly alive to the fact
that those who think they have got some new light

are often merely pursuing *ignes fatui.* 'Nor yet,' he adds, 'do I desire to belong to that class of men who cling to the old and the customary, spite of the indications of God Himself, Reason, and Common Sense.'[1]

Out of the Moravian evangelical soil he grew, and a Moravian in heart and soul he remained to the end. It is important to note this. We have already pointed out in the Introduction that the educational motive was in the first Reformation age—that of Luther and Melanchthon,—partly literary or Humanistic, but chiefly religious or theological: in the second Reformation age, to which Comenius belonged, the intense conflict of opinion between the new and the old faith—made keener by the reaction to Catholicism under the influence mainly of the Jesuits—had driven the Humanistic element to the wall, and the theological aim in education now almost wholly obscured the literary. The torch of reason, lighted in the schools half a century previously, was now darkened by the smoke of theological contentions and disastrous wars. Comenius was, above all things, a genuine representative of the evangelical spirit; he was not afraid of science—far from it: he endeavoured to unite science and theology, —but he did not fairly appreciate Humanism, and accepted the products of the genius of past ages only in a half-hearted way. His eyes were turned to the present and the future.

At sixteen Comenius went, or was sent, to a Latin school, and in 1612, when he was twenty years of age, we find him at the College of Herborn, in the duke-

[1] *Lectoribus,* vol. i.

dom of Nassau, pursuing his theological studies under Professor Alsted, afterwards Professor of Theology and Philosophy at Weissenburg. To the lateness of the age at which he began Latin we probably partly owe Comenius's early insight into the defects of educational methods. He was old enough to criticise, while submitting to, the scholastic discipline and defective modes of procedure, of which he was, with others, the victim. There is no reason to believe that his school was worse than schools elsewhere at that time, and of these he says that 'they are the terror of boys, and the slaughter-houses of minds,—places where a hatred of literature and books is contracted, where ten or more years are spent in learning what might be acquired in one, where what ought to be poured in gently is violently forced in and beaten in, where what ought to be put clearly and perspicuously is presented in a confused and intricate way, as if it were a collection of puzzles,—places where minds are fed on words.' Well might Professor Lubinus of Rostock say that the instruction and discipline of schools seemed to have been the invention of some wicked spirit, the enemy of the human race. 'Millibus e multis,' he exclaims, 'ego quoque sum unus, miser homuncio, cui amœnissimum vitæ ver, florentes juventutis anni, nugis scholasticis transmissi, misere perierunt. Ah, quoties mihi postquam melius prospicere datum, perditae aetatis recordatio, pectore suspiria, oculis lacrymas, corde dolorem excussit. Ah, quoties me dolor ille exclamare coegit—

'O mihi praeteritos referat si Jupiter annos.'

Before Comenius left school, Ratich, of whom we have already spoken, was at work; and it was in 1612, when Comenius was still at Herborn, that the public document issued by the Universities of Jena and Giessen, commenting on Ratich's proposed innovations, first came under his notice.[1] The Ratichian scheme, on which specially the University laudation was pronounced, was printed under the following title: *Wolphgangi Ratichii de Studiorum rectificanda methodo Consilium.*

Comenius was profoundly attracted by the new educational movement.

After a year or more spent in travel, during which he resided at Amsterdam and studied at Heidelberg, he returned to his native Moravia in 1614. Being now twenty-two years of age, and being still too young for the ministry, he was appointed Rector of the Moravian school at Prærovium (Prerau), near Olmütz, where he at once endeavoured to introduce improved methods of instruction and a more humane discipline.

'Ten years,' he says,[2] 'are given to the study of the Latin tongue, and after all the result is disappointing. Erasmus, Vives, Luther, Sturm, Frisch, Sanctius, Domavius, have all complained of this. Boyhood is distracted,' he goes on to say, 'for years with precepts of grammar, infinitely prolix, perplexed, and obscure, and for the most part useless. Boys are stuffed with vocabularies without associating words with things, or indeed with one another syntactically.' It had been

[1] Preface to vol. i.
[2] Preface to first edition of the *Janua Linguarum.*

hoped that the substitution for barbarous Latinity of good authors, such as Terence, Cicero, Virgil, and Horace—the work of the Humanists,—would cure the universal evil by teaching boys the Latin tongue by means of its purest writers. But this had failed, partly because of the unpropitiousness of the time, but chiefly because the secret of education lies in method, and in the master who wields it. No attempt had been made to secure either sound method or good masters. What else but failure could be expected?

At Prerau Comenius began by simplifying the Latin Grammar, and wrote an elementary book for his pupils, which was afterwards published at Prague in 1616 (*Grammaticae facilioris praecepta*).

In this year he was ordained to the pastorate, but whether this caused him to give up the school does not appear.[1] He was not appointed to any special charge till 1618, when he was set over 'the most flourishing of all the churches of the Moravian Brethren, that of Fulneck,' near Troppau. Along with his ministerial charge, he had the superintendence of a school recently erected ; and he now began to consider more fully the subject of instruction, and to put his thoughts on paper.[2] Here too he married, and for two or three years spent a happy and active life, enjoying the only period of tranquillity in his native country which it was ever his fortune to experience. For the restoration of a time so happy he never ceased to pine during all his future wanderings.

---

[1] Dedication to *Schola Ludus*, vol. iii. p. 831.
[2] Preface to vol. i.

The Thirty Years' War broke out, and in 1621 Fulneck was taken by the Spaniards, and all the property of Comenius destroyed, including his library and manuscripts.[1] For the next three years Comenius seems to have resided, along with several other Moravian pastors, under the protection of Karl von Zerotin, a wealthy. Moravian, and while there wrote a book entitled *The Labyrinth of the World and the Paradise of the Heart,* an allegorical writing on the vanity of earthly things.[2] In 1622 he lost his wife and only child. In 1624 he and his fellow-pastors were compelled to leave the protection of Zerotin, and thereafter, evading as best they could the persecution of the Jesuits, they wandered through various parts of Moravia and Bohemia, occasionally visiting their communities secretly, and preaching the Word and administering the Sacraments.

In July 1627 the evangelical pastors in Moravia and Bohemia were formally proscribed by the Austrian Government, acting under the instigation of the Jesuits. Some took refuge among the Bohemian mountains with Baron Sadouski von Slaupna. To one of the pastors who took refuge there—John Stadius by name—the Baron intrusted his three sons for their education. For the benefit of the tutor, and at his request, Comenius wrote some rules of method. In the autumn of that

---

[1] Seyffart says that on this occasion he lost also his wife and two children, but Comenius himself does not mention this in his Preface to vol. i. Seyffart has doubtless other authority for what he says. I confine myself solely to what can be ascertained by collating Comenius's own writings.

[2] Printed at Lissa in 1631.

year he paid a visit to Wilcitz, not far off, to look at the
library there. Among the books, he unexpectedly met
with the treatise of Elias Bodinus, recently imported
from Germany, and was fired with the ambition to produce a like work in his own Bohemian tongue. In this
ambition he was sustained by the approval, and indeed
solicitations, of his fellow-refugees, who were convinced
that he had much to say that would be of value to
schools and schoolmasters. While engaged in this
didactic work, he was disturbed by a new edict requiring all the evangelical pastors to renounce their faith, or
finally leave the country. Churches and schools were
ruthlessly destroyed. Comenius from his retreat was a
witness from time to time of the acts of the persecutors,
and was overwhelmed with grief. He still, however,
desired to live within reach of the brethren of his
community, and did not leave the mountains, where
he thought he might possibly escape observation. His
active and practical mind began at once to consider
how he should proceed to restore religion and piety
should he ever be free again to work for his native
country. His didactic studies suggested to him that
the great agency for a future renovation lay in schools,
and he consoled himself with this reflection, and with
forming sanguine schemes for the future. His sole
desire now was to devote his life entirely to the young,
should it please God to restore him to his country, and
by the institution of schools, by supplying them with
good books, and with a simple and lucid method, to
build up, more surely than before, learning, virtue, and

piety.   Meanwhile by secret communications with his
brethren he tried to sustain their sinking spirits.   The
persecution, however, waxed hotter, and finding it impossible longer to continue in his concealment, he and
his companions fled, dispersing in different directions.
Comenius made for Poland, which he had once before
visited on a secret mission, having been sent thither
by the Moravian Brethren—probably in order to ascertain if they could find an asylum in that country.   He
betook himself to the town of *Lesna* (Lissa, Leszno), in
Posnania, and obtained employment as a teacher in the
Moravian Gymnasium there—apparently as Rector of
it.[1]   The Count of Lissa (Rafael) afforded protection to
the persecuted brethren.   His scholastic engagements,
and the desire to do his duty in an efficient way, gave a
fresh impulse to his didactic studies.   He began to re-
construct his methods from the foundation, and to give
them a philosophic basis and a logical coherence.

Not only had the general question of Education
engaged many minds for a century and more before
Comenius arose, but the apparently subsidiary, yet all-
important, question of *Method*, in special relation to the
teaching of the Latin tongue, had occupied the thoughts
and pens of many of the leading scholars of Europe.   The
whole field of what we now call Secondary Instruction
was occupied with the one subject of Latin ; Greek, and

---

[1] In the *Dictionnaire de Pédagogie* his scholastic function is
described as being that of organiser of the education of the
Moravian Colony only.   That his duties were of a more general
kind is clear from his own writings.

occasionally Hebrew, having been admitted only in the beginning of the sixteenth century, and then only to a subordinate place. This of necessity. Latin was the one key to universal learning. To give to boys the possession of this key was all that teachers aimed at until their pupils were old enough to study Rhetoric and Logic. Of these writers on the teaching of Latin, the most eminent were Sturm, Erasmus, Melanchthon, Lubinus, Vossius, Sanctius (the author of the *Minerva*), Ritter, Helvicus, Bodinus, Valentinus Andreæ, and, among Frenchmen, Cœcilius Frey.[1] Nor were Ascham and Mulcaster in England the least significant of the critics of Method. Comenius was acquainted with almost all previous writers on education, except probably Ascham and Mulcaster, to whom he never alludes. He read everything that he could hear of with a view to find a method, and he does not appear ever to have been desirous to supersede the work of others. If he had found what he wanted, he would, we believe, have promulgated it, and advocated it as a loyal pupil. That he owed much to previous writers is certain; but the prime characteristic of his work on Latin was his own. Especially does he introduce a new epoch in education, by constructing a general methodology which should go beyond mere Latin, and be equally applicable to all subjects of instruction.

Before bringing his thoughts into definite shape, he

---

[1] Frey published at Paris in 1629 an educational treatise entitled *Ad divas scientias, artesque, et linguas sermonesque extemporaneos nova et expeditissima* [*via*].

wrote to all the distinguished men to whom he could obtain access. He addressed Ratich, among others, but received no answer; many of his letters also were returned, because the persons addressed could not be found.[1] Valentinus Andreæ wrote to him in encouraging terms, saying that he gladly passed on the torch to him. His mind became now much agitated by the importance of the question, and by the excitement of discovery. He saw his whole scheme assuming shape under his pen, and was filled, like other zealous men, before and since, with the highest hopes of the benefits which he would confer on the whole human race by his discoveries. He resolved to call his treatise *Didactica Magna*, or *Omnes omnia docendi Artificium*. He found a consolation for his misfortunes in the work of invention, and even saw the hand of Providence in the coincidence of the overthrow of schools, through persecutions and wars, and those ideas of a new method which had been vouchsafed to him, and which he was elaborating. Everything might now be begun anew, and untrammelled by the errors and prejudices of the past. Some scruples as to a theologian and pastor being so entirely preoccupied with educational questions, he had however to overcome.[2] 'Suffer, I pray, Christian friends, that I speak confidentially with you for a moment. Those who know me intimately, know that I am a man of moderate ability, and of almost no learning, but one

---

[1] Among his correspondents were Sigmund Evenius, Abraham Mencel, Paliurus, Jonston, Mochinger, Docem, George Winkler, Martin Moser, and Niclassius.

[2] *Lectoribus*, vol. i. p. 7.

who, bewailing the evils of his time, is eager to remedy them, if this in any way be granted me to do, either by my own discoveries or by those of another—none of which things can come save from a gracious God. If, then, anything be here found well done, it is not mine, but His, who from the mouths of babes and sucklings hath perfected praise, and who, that He may in verity show Himself faithful, true, and gracious, gives to those who ask, opens to those who knock, and offers to those who seek. Christ my Lord knows that my heart is so simple that it matters not to me whether I teach or be taught, act the part of teacher of teachers, or disciple of disciples. What the Lord has given me I send forth for the common good.' His deepest conviction was that the sole hope of healing the dissensions of both Church and State lay in the proper education of youth. The τεχνὴ τεχνῶν ἄνθρωπον ἄγειν of Gregory Nazianzen was with him a favourite quotation. At the same time, he did not profess, as we have said, to supersede all others: on the contrary, he truly and wisely says, 'Artem artium tradere operosae molis res est, exquisitoque eget judicio; nec unius hominis sed multorum, quum unus nemo tam sit oculatus cujus aciem non subterfugiant plurima.'

When he had completed his *Great Didactic*, he did not publish it, for he was still hoping to be restored to his native Moravia, where he proposed to execute all his philanthropic schemes ; indeed, the treatise was first written in his native Sclav or Czech tongue.[1]

---

[1] Found in the archives of Lissa in 1841, and republished in its Czech form in 1849 by a Bohemian Society.

While thus engaged in working out his theory and method of education, Comenius had been searching for some elementary Latin reading-book, which might introduce boys easily to the use of the Latin tongue.

In addition to the defects already universally recognised in the teaching of Latin, Comenius pointed out that, even supposing the usual classical authors were read and mastered, a boy would not then know the Latin words expressing the things and ideas of his own time. 'Finally, if so much time is to be spent on the language alone,' he says, 'when is the boy to know about things—when will he learn philosophy, when religion, and so forth? He will consume his life in preparing for life.' Some epitome of the language is wanted, in which the words and phrases will be reduced to one body, as it were, and in this way much time saved in acquiring them. For, as Isaac Habrecht truly said, one would learn to know all the animals of the world more quickly by visiting Noah's ark than by traversing the world and picking up knowledge as we went.

To meet this want, a member of the Irish College of Salamanca (Bateus by name) had written a *Janua Linguarum*, comprising in one lesson-book all the more usual words, and these connected into sentences so constructed that no vocable occurred more than once, except such indispensable words as *sum, et, in*, etc. This book was in Latin-Spanish, and was shortly after, in 1615, published in Latin-English in London. Two years after Isaac Habrecht of Strasbourg published a

Latin-Spanish-English-French edition, and so made it quadrilingual, and on his return to Germany added a German version, strongly commending it as an excellent means of learning a language. The work was frequently republished in many parts of Germany, was introduced into many schools, and ultimately, in 1629, appeared in eight languages.

At first Comenius hailed this book with pleasure, but after carefully studying it, came to the conclusion that it did not justify its title; and this, *first*, because it contained many words beyond the capacity of the young, while omitting many in daily use; *secondly*, because the words, which were used only once, were used in one signification only, whereas they constantly, in native authors, have more than one meaning, and thus pupils are misled; and *thirdly*, because, where one signification is alone given, it ought always to be the primary one, which in the book in question was not the case. There were other objections to the book: the sentences did not contribute to the moral instruction of youth, and were clumsy, and, indeed, even often destitute of meaning.

'My fundamental principle—an irrefragable law of didactics—is,' he says, in speaking of his own *Janua*, 'that the understanding and the tongue should advance in parallel lines always. The human being tends to utter what he apprehends. If he does not apprehend the words he uses, he is a parrot; if he apprehends without words, he is a dumb statue. Accordingly, under 100 heads, I have classified the whole uni-

C

verse of things in a manner suited to the capacity of boys, and I have given the corresponding language.   I have selected from Lexicons the words that had to be introduced, and I include 8000 vocables in 1000 sentences, which are at first simple, and thereafter gradually become complex.   I have used words, as far as practicable, in their primary signification, according to the comprehension of the young, but have had to seek for modern Latin words where pure Latin was not to be had.   I have used the same word only once, except where it had two meanings.   Synonyms and contraries I have placed together, so that they may throw light on one another.   I have arranged the words so as to bring into view concords and governments and declension. The vernacular text (Czech or Bohemian) I have printed separately on this occasion, as it would be useless to many whose judgments on my effort I desire to have.   An index of the words (not however, absolutely necessary) will be afterwards added; also a brief treatise on homonyms, synonyms, etc., and a short, compendious, simple, and easy grammar—all of which, comprised in one volume, will be a little treasure-house of school-learning.'

Three years were spent on the *Janua* alone, and yet Comenius was far from thinking the work perfect: he considered he had only led the way for others.   He hoped also himself, from time to time, to improve the book.

He called this little book a 'Seminary of Tongues and all Sciences,' because equal care had been given to *things* and *words*.   He desired to introduce some beginnings and clear perception of things, and at the same time to lay the foundations of learning, morals, and piety.

Speaking generally, we may say that Comenius's aim was—*first*, to simplify and graduate ; *secondly*, to teach words through things ; *thirdly*, to teach things through words. The book was a very remarkable innovation on the then existing school text-books ; but, notwithstanding this, or because of it, when he published it in 1631, at the urgent solicitation of his friends, and before, in his opinion, it was perfected, it achieved an immediate and enormous success. 'People,' he says,[1] 'seemed to vie with one another in producing editions of it.' It was translated into Greek, Bohemian, Polish, German, Swedish, Belgian, English, French, Spanish, Italian, Hungarian, Turkish, Arabic, and into a language which he calls Mogolic, 'and which,' he says, ' was familiar to the populations of India.' He next, in 1633, published his *Vestibulum*, which was intended to serve as an easy introduction to the *Janua*.

In 1632 there was convened a synod of the Moravian Brethren at Lissa, at which Comenius (now forty years of age) was elected to succeed his father-in-law Cyrillus as Bishop of the scattered brethren—a position which enabled him to be of great service, by means of correspondence, to the members of the community, who were dispersed in various parts of Europe. Throughout the whole of his long life he continued this fatherly charge, and seemed never quite to abandon the hope

[1] Dedication of *Schola Ludus*, vol. iii.

of being restored, along with his fellow-exiles, to his native land—a hope doomed to disappointment. In his capacity of Pastor-Bishop he wrote several treatises, such as a *History of the Persecutions of the Brotherhood*, an account of the *Moravian Church-discipline and Order*, and polemical tracts against a contemporary Socinian.

Meanwhile his great Didactic treatise, which had been written in his native Czech tongue, was yet unpublished. He was, it would appear, stimulated to the publication of it by an invitation he received in 1638, from the authorities in Sweden, to visit their country and undertake the reformation of their schools.[1] He replied that he was unwilling to undertake a task at once so onerous and so invidious, but that he would gladly give the benefit of his advice to any one of their own nation whom they might select for the duty. These communications led him to resume his labour on the Great Didactic, and to translate it into Latin, in which form it finally appeared.[2]

In education Comenius was a Sense-Realist—the first great and thoroughly consistent Realist. Von Raumer says :—'He received his first impulse in this direction, as he himself relates, from the well-known Spanish pedagogue Ludovic Vives, who declared himself against Aristotle, and demanded a Christian instead of a heathen mode of philosophising.' 'It is not disputation

---

[1] Preface to vol. i.

[2] I cannot find the precise date. In the *Dictionnaire de Pédagogie* it is stated that the work, though completed at the time stated in the above, was not published till 1657. I think this is a mistake.

which leads to any result,' said Vives, 'but the silent observation of Nature. It is better for the scholars to ask questions and to investigate than to be disputing with each other.' 'Yet,' says Comenius, 'Vives understood better where the fault lay than what was the remedy.'

Comenius received a second impulse from Thomas Campanella, who, however, did not satisfy him. 'But when,' he says, 'Bacon's *Instauratio Magna* came into my hands—a wonderful work, which I consider the most instructive philosophical work of the century now beginning,—I saw in it that Campanella's demonstrations are wanting in that thoroughness which is demanded by the truth of things. Yet again I was troubled, because the noble Verulam, while giving the true key of Nature, did not unlock her secrets, but only showed, by a few examples, how they should be unlocked, and left the rest to future observations to be extended through centuries.' He goes on, in the preface to the *Physics*, from which these utterances are taken, to say that he is convinced that it is not Aristotle who must be master of philosophy for Christians, but that philosophy must be studied fully according to the leading of sense, reason, and books. 'For,' he continues, 'do *we* not dwell in the garden of Nature as well as the ancients? Why should we not use our eyes, ears, and noses as well as they? And why should we need other teachers than these our senses to learn to know the works of Nature? Why, say I, should we not, instead of these dead books, lay open the living book of Nature, in which there is much more to contemplate than any one person can ever relate, and the contemplation of which brings much more of pleasure, as well as of profit?' It is this realism which explains his school-books and also his method.

It was natural that the strong realistic impulse should travel beyond the sphere of schools, and cause men to dream of great things. The *Advancement of Learning* had filled Comenius, as well as other contemporary men, with hopes of a rapid and unparalleled progress in all the sciences, and a consequent improvement of the conditions of human life. With a view to a thorough co-ordination and universal diffusion of scientific know-ledge, he contemplated the issuing of a complete body of science as then understood. To effect this, the com-bination of many minds, each in its own department, and all under the guidance of some controlling intellect, was necessary. Men were working in various parts of Europe independently of each other, and, the younger men especially, in ignorance of what had been actually accomplished in the sciences to which they devoted themselves. An exhaustive but concise and authori-tative statement of all that was known in each depart-ment could not fail to be of immense service, and, as Comenius thought, for his mind was always practical, of great influence on the progress and well-being of society. This complete statement of the circle of knowledge he called *Pansophia*, and it was in this direction that his real life-work lay, in his own opinion; his scholastic under-takings being strictly subordinate to the greater task.

Although not prepared to give effect to his views in proper form, he had been working at the Pansophy in the retirement of his study during the years which saw the completion of the first edition of his *Janua* and of his *Great Didactic.* In the department of Science he had already given to the world a treatise on Astronomy and on the reforming of Physics (1633). He had also, by correspondence, interested various learned men in his encyclopædic or pansophic scheme : among others, Samuel Hartlib, the friend of Milton, who was then resident in London, and to whom Milton addressed his tractate on Education.

'Everybody knew Hartlib,' says Professor Masson in his *Life of Milton* (vol. iii. p. 193). 'He was a foreigner by birth, being the son of a Polish merchant of German extraction, who had left Poland when that country fell under Jesuit rule, and had settled in Elbing in Prussia in very good circumstances. Twice married before to Polish ladies, this merchant had married in Prussia, for his third wife, the daughter of a wealthy English merchant of Dantzic; and thus our Hartlib, their son, though Prussian born, and with Polish connections, could reckon himself half-English. The date of his birth was probably about the beginning of the century, *i.e.* he may have been eight or ten years older than Milton. He appears to have first visited England in or about 1628, and from that time, though he made frequent journeys to the Continent, London had been his head-quarters. Here, with a residence in the City, he had carried on business as a "merchant," with

extensive foreign correspondences and very respectable
family connections. . . . But it did not require such
family connections to make Hartlib at home in English
society.   The character of the man would have made
him at home anywhere.   He was one of those persons
now styled "philanthropists," or "friends of progress,"
who take an interest in every question or project of
their time promising social improvement, have always
some iron in the fire, are constantly forming committees
or writing letters to persons of influence, and altogether
live for the public.   By the common consent of all who
have explored the intellectual and social history of
England in the seventeenth century, he is one of the
most interesting and memorable figures of that whole
period.   He is interesting both for what he did himself,
and also on account of the number and intimacy of his
contacts with other interesting people[1].'   Hartlib was
not slow to be interested in the educational ideas of
Comenius, but he was specially inspired by the two
leading projects of the time—the Union of Protestant
Christendom, and, by help of this, the settlement of
nations, and the union of the sciences in a complete
encyclopædic form.   Comenius, at his request, had sent
him a long epistle, setting forth in full his Pansophic
project, and this epistle was printed at Oxford in 1637,
without Comenius's consent, and widely circulated.   The
treatise was called by Hartlib *Porta Sapientiae reserata.*
It is entitled by Comenius in the List of Contents (*vide*
Collected Works) *Prodromus Pansophiae* (Precursor of
Pansophy) and in the body of his works, *Pansophiae*

---

[1] See Note, p. 229.

praeludium, quo Sapientiae universalis necessitas, possi-
bilitas facilitasque (si rationè certa incatur) breviter ac
dilucidè demonstratur. The running head-title of the
treatise again is *Pansophici Libri Delineatio.* To meet
the objections of critics, Comenius shortly after wrote a
brief treatise further expounding his views, entitled
Conatuum pansophicorum dilucidatio in gratiam Cen-
sorum facta (1638).

These treatises excited much interest throughout
Europe. Adolph Tassius, Professor of Mathematics at
Hamburg, wrote to Hartlib[1] saying,—'A philosophic
ardour flames in every corner of Europe, and with it
zeal for a better Didactic. If Comenius had done
nothing more than scatter such fruitful seeds in the
minds of all, he would have done enough.'

The reception accorded to the Pansophic ideas of
Comenius was encouraging enough, but it was apparent
to all, and to none more than Comenius, that they
could be carried out only by a community or college of
learned men, and that this college would have to be
a permanent institution for the furtherance of science,
and for the authoritative promulgation from time to time
of the scientific *status quo.* A Collegium Didacticum
or Pansophicum was accordingly projected. It might
have been urged that the Universities existed for these
very purposes, but it is (it appears to me) a mistake to
suppose that these institutions had as yet thought of the
prosecution of science as the main end of their institution. Except in so far as they were seminaries of
' Disputations,' they were to a large extent merely higher

[1] Vol. i. p. 455.

academies for giving instruction to qualify for the various
faculties and professions; and to convert them into
centres of scientific research and illumination would
not have been in those days possible, although it would
have been quite in harmony with their original design.
It is only in recent times that the purely scientific idea
has found its way into the heart of the University
system, and that Professors are expected to represent
and advance their subject as well as to afford instruction
in it to all comers. The combination of the scientific
with the teaching function constitutes, indeed, the ideal
of a University system.   There was, in the beginning
of the seventeenth century, no way open to Comenius
and his friends save by the foundation of an entirely
new institution.   For this, money was wanted, and also
influential support.

At the urgent solicitation of the sanguine Hartlib,
who had been busying himself among members of the
Long Parliament, Comenius repaired to London, which
he reached on the 22d September 1641.   There he
found that he had been invited by Parliament itself;
but as it was prorogued for a few months owing to King
Charles's absence in Scotland, he had to wait.   He
employed his time well in expounding his views to
various people of influence, and on the re-assembling
of Parliament he was asked to wait a little longer until
a commission of learned men could be appointed to
inquire into his proposals.   Parliament even went so
far as to propose to set apart the revenues and buildings
of a college in London, or Winchester, or Chelsea, to

which men might be called from various parts of the
world and maintained in residence while prosecuting
their learned researches and giving effect to Comenius's
great Pansophic scheme. A statement of the revenues
of Chelsea College was even placed in Comenius's
hands, and he now began to entertain lively expecta-
tions that ere long the ideas of the great Verulam would
be realised, and a 'universal college opened, solely
devoted to the advancement of the sciences.' The
general unsettlement of affairs, aggravated by the Irish
rebellion and the massacre of the Protestants, did not
admit, however, of the carrying out of any peaceful
project. The country was on the eve of rebellion, and
the leaders in Parliament could scarcely be expected to
find time for any save the greatest national and political
affairs. Everything was in confusion, and Comenius,
deeply disappointed, prepared to return to the Continent.

It was precisely at this moment that he received, from
a correspondent and admirer in Sweden, a letter which
led him to change his plans. The name of this friend,
who plays an important part in Comenius's future life,
was Ludovic de Geer, a man of noble family, of considerable wealth, and, happily, also of an enlightened
and progressive mind. He was a Dutchman settled
in Sweden. He assured Comenius that his personal
influence would enable him to promote his views in
Sweden (at that time ruled by Christina and the famous
Chancellor Oxenstiern), and that he could secure the
co-operation of others. In accepting this invitation,
Comenius had the approval of his English friends, but as

De Geer had evidently in view the Didactic rather than the Pansophic innovations of Comenius, they protested by anticipation against his being drawn aside from what they considered to be the larger aim to the more restricted subject of school-books.

Comenius left London for Sweden in August 1642 and was kindly received by De Geer at Nordköping.[1] After a few days spent with his host, he was sent on to Stockholm with introductions to Oxenstiern and to John Skyte, Chancellor of the University of Upsala. By both he was treated with respect, and his plans, Pansophic and Didactic, fully discussed. Of his interviews Comenius himself gives an account in the Preface to the second volume of his works. 'For four days,' he says, 'these two men held me in debate, but chiefly Oxenstiern, that eagle of the North (Aquilonaris Aquila), who questioned me as to my principles, both Pansophic and Didactic, with a greater penetration and closeness than had been exhibited by any of the learned with whom I had come in contact. For the first three days Didactic was the subject of his examination, and he brought the interviews to an end with the following remarks : "From youth up I have perceived a certain violence in the customary method of school studies, but I could never put my finger on the place where the shoe pinched. When sent by my King, of glorious memory,[2] as an ambassador to Germany, I conferred with many learned men on the subject; and when I

---

[1] On the Baltic, eighty-five miles south-west of Stockholm.
[2] Gustavus Adolphus.

was informed that Wolfgang Ratich had attempted a
reform of Method, I had no peace in my mind till I had
the man before me ; but he, instead of a conversation,
presented me with a huge book in quarto. I swallowed
that annoyance, and having run through the whole
volume, I saw that he had exposed the diseases of
schools not badly, but as for the remedies, they did not
seem to me to be adequate. Your remedies rest on
firmer foundations ; go on with your work," etc. To
which I replied that in these matters I had done what I
could, and that now I wished to pass to other matters.
His answer was : "I know that you are undertaking
greater things, for I have read the Prodromus of your
Pansophia, and on this point we shall talk to-morrow, for
public duties now call me elsewhere." On the following
day, when about to examine my Pansophic labours, but
with a greater aspect of severity, he prefaced his
examination with this question : "Can you bear contradiction?" "I can," I replied. "The Prodromus was
published not by me but by my friends, for the very
purpose of receiving opinions and criticisms : and
if we admit these from any and every quarter, of whatsoever kind, why not from men of matured wisdom and
of eminent judgment?" He then began to speak
against the hopes I had conceived of a better state of
things as likely to arise from a rightly instituted
Pansophic study, first making political objections of
profound import, and then bringing forward the testimony of Holy Writ, which seems to predict that darkness
and degeneracy rather than light and an improved

state of society would prevail towards the end of the world. My replies he received in the spirit indicated by his concluding remarks : "To no one yet, I think, have such things occurred. Stand on these foundations, for either we shall reach a consensus of opinion in the way you propose, or it will be made clear that there is no way. Nevertheless my advice is that you devote yourself first to benefit schools and to make the study of Latin easier, and by that means to prepare a smoother way for the greater things."'

The Chancellor of the University added the weight of his advice to the same effect, suggesting that Comenius should move to a locality near Sweden, such as Elbing on the Baltic coast of Prussia. Finding that his friend De Geer was of the same mind, he yielded, in the hope of bringing these troublesome and vexatious toils to a close in a year or two. When he communicated his resolution to his friends in England, he received a strong protest. They complained of his too great facility in yielding to his Swedish advisers, and of his unfaithfulness to the great Pansophic scheme. 'Quo moriture ruis?' wrote Hartlib. 'Minoraque viribus audes?' He was much shaken by these representations — the more, that they supported his own real inclinations. A Swedish remonstrance, however, reached him at Lesna, which finally determined him to go to Elbing and prosecute his Didactic labours. To these he now devoted himself, after first putting to press, in 1643, at Danzig, a treatise on Pansophia, entitled *Pansophiae Diatyposis, Ichnographica et Ortho-*

graphica, a work afterwards republished at Amsterdam and Paris.

When, in his retirement at Elbing, where he was supported by De Geer, he had laboured at his Didactic treatises for nearly four years—'rolling his Sisyphæan stone,' as he calls it—he again visited Sweden (1646) with his manuscripts, and having submitted them to a commission of three judges, was directed to publish them as soon as he had given them his last touches. Two years, however, of hard labour on the Lexicons and Grammars which were to accompany his books still awaited him, and it was only in 1648 that he was in a position to publish. At this time he returned to his Polish home at Lesna, the proper centre of his episcopal work, and at the Lesna press the fruits of his labours were printed.

A complete list of the works which were the fruit of those six years' labours will be found at the end of this memoir, under their proper titles. They included the most elaborate of all his treatises on Method, except his Great Didactic, viz., *The Newest Method of Languages solidly based on Didactic Foundations*, and a specimen of a *Vestibulum*, for the final shape of which he refers his readers to the *Vestibulum* afterwards revised at Patak in Hungary : also a new edition of the *Janua*, for which also his readers are referred to its final and completed form as revised at Patak :[1] a Latin-vernacular Grammar

---

[1] Both *Vestibulum* and *Janua* were, however, printed at Lesna before he went to Patak, as appears from vol. iii. in the Dedicatory Epistle prefixed to the *Schola Ludus.*

for the *Janua*, with appended annotations for the use of teachers—a very clear, complete, and yet brief work compared with the Grammars of the time ; and a Latin-German Lexicon, published later, in 1656, at Frankfort, and not included in the collected works, as being too cumbrous. A more advanced school-book, entitled *Atrium Linguae Latinae*, he had just begun when he was called into Hungary, where it was completed. The imperfections of these books, as indeed of all his writings, he is always ready to admit, pleading that no one man could all at once correct the mistakes of the past, place education on a right basis, and furnish the school with proper instruments of teaching.

While still engaged in the completion of the works which belong to this Elbing period, when he was subsidised by De Geer, he received many testimonies from men high in position as to the value of his labours. An interesting correspondence with the Palatine of *Posnania*, 'Christoph. Opalinski de Bnin,' himself an author and a vigorous promoter of education in his own country, was lost in the destruction of Lesna by the Swedish army, in 1655, under Charles x.—an invasion which destroyed also the gymnasium at Sirakovia, which Opalinski had founded and supplied with translations of Comenius's school-books.[1]

The products of the six years of Elbing industry he dedicated to De Geer.

Having discharged his obligations to his Swedish

---

[1] *Judicia, novaeque disquisitiones.*—Vol. ii. of *Works*, p. 458.

friends in the department of Didactics, he was about now, at last, to apply himself exclusively to the greater Pansophic schemes, and was contemplating future labours in this direction with much complacency when he received a letter from the Prince Sigismund Racocus,[1] and his widowed mother, the Princess of Transylvania, urging him to advise in the reformation of the schools in their country. The requests of mother and son were enforced by communications from theologians, and were favourably entertained by him because of the kindness shown in Transylvania to exiled Moravians. Accordingly, in May 1650, he betook himself to Saros-Patak, a market-town of Hungary, on the Bodrogh, and thence, along with their Highnesses, to Tokay, twenty miles to the north-east. It was in this year that he published his *Lux in Tenebris*, a book on the fulfilment of modern prophecy, and became entangled with one Drabicius,[2] who gave himself out as a prophet and gained a certain following. This weakness in Comenius may be touched with a gentle hand. His theological writings show that he had strong mystical leanings, and in later life he was a devoted admirer of Madame Bourignon, to whom, indeed, he stood in personal relations.

The form which his scholastic labours now took com-

[1] George I., Ragotzski, Prince of Transylvania. This country was not incorporated in the Austrian dominions till 1699. Hungary accrued to Austria in 1526, and became hereditary in 1687.

[2] For an account of Drabicius and Kotterus, see Bayle's *Dictionary*. Their productions were largely embodied in Comenius's book. The date of the *publication* of *Lux in Tenebris* is given variously. This is doubtless due to the confounding of the Czech and Latin editions.

bined the Didactic with the Pansophic more fully than hitherto. Being asked to put his idea of a Pansophic school in writing, he printed his *Illustris Scholae Patakinae Idea*, and thereafter in full detail his *Scholae Pansophicae classibus septem adornandae Delineatio.* During his residence at Patak, which lasted till 1654, he produced fifteen works, among which were the new editions of the *Vestibulum* and *Janua*, the first edition of the *Atrium*, the famous *Orbis Pictus* (World Illustrated),[1] and the *Schola Ludus.*

These text-books are described in the account of Comenius's educational views which follows this sketch of his life and labours. The most characteristic and important of the works of this period was the *Schola Pansophica*, or *Universalis Sapientiae Officina*, an account of which will also be found in its proper place. He desired to make the new Patak seminary not merely a Pansophic school, but also to give it the character of a Latin state, nay, even of Latium itself. Nothing but Latin was to be spoken.[2] This was practicable, because he contemplated a college in which all the pupils should dwell together.

His patrons did all they could to fulfil their promises of support. They gave him a collegiate building, and, in addition to this, they purchased the fourth house from the college for the school. Comenius's plan was to buy up the intervening houses, with their gardens, and as many on the other side, so as to provide resi-

---

[1] Printed at Nüremberg in 1658.
[2] *Deliberatio de Latio a Tiberi ad Brodrocum transferendo.*

dences for seven masters, and also seven class-rooms. The whole was to be surrounded by a continuous wall, so that a little Latin state (*Latina civitatula*) might be planted, with its own open areas and gardens—all enclosed from the outer world. This was to be a little republic, having its own customs, laws, judges, and senate, and its own chapel and services. The masters were to preside over a large family like fathers, and there, in a course of seven years, beginning at the age of twelve, boys were to be instructed in 'all things that perfect human nature,' and trained to be pious Christians and wise and cultivated men.

The three-class school which formed the lower division of this Pansophic seminary was organised with a view to instruction in Latin along with Real things. The higher classes, up to the seventh, are described elsewhere. They do not seem ever to have been organised.

The Precepts of Manners, collected for the use of youth in 1653, are amusing, and at the same time afford evidence of the exaggerated conceptions which Comenius entertained of the possibilities of education. He believed, in truth, that he could manufacture a man. These also were written for the Patak school.

The *Schola Ludus*, which is a kind of dramatic *Janua Linguarum et Rerum*, was likewise written and printed for the Patak school. An elaborate Latino-latin Lexicon was also composed during the four years' residence at Patak. Comenius left it behind him in MS., and it was afterwards printed at Amsterdam in 1657.

The Prince Sigismund, unfortunately, died prema-

turely, and those in authority after his death resolved
to limit the new institution to the three-class Latin, or
philological, school, and for the use of this school the
Vestibulum, Janua, and *Atrium* were printed in Latin-
Hungarian.   The Patak school was auspiciously opened
under three carefully selected masters, and Comenius
believed it to be flourishing in 1657, when, at Amsterdam, he was writing his dedicatory epistle prefixed to
the *Schola Ludus*.   It had, however, suffered from the
plague of 1655, which temporarily broke it up.   Having
accomplished his work of organisation and book-writing,
Comenius left Hungary in 1654, pronouncing his vale-
dictory address on June 2d of that year, in presence of
a distinguished assembly.[1]

In that address he informs his audience that his
objects in school reform were—to give compendiums
for learning the Latin tongue, which would make the
acquisition of it pleasant; to introduce a higher and
better philosophy into school work, so as to fit youth
for the investigation of the causes of things; and to
create a higher tone of morals and manners.   To carry
out these objects, he had constructed, he tells them,
a *Vestibulum* and a *Janua* of the Latin tongue for the
first two classes, with their accompanying lexicons and
grammars, and an *Atrium* for the third stage, with a
more extended grammar, including idioms, phrases, and
elegancies, and a Latino-latin lexicon.   As to science,
arts, philosophy, morals, and theology, he had so con-

[1] *Laborum Scholasticorum Patakini obitorum Coroniso,* vide
vol. iii. p. 1041.

structed the above-named books that they contained
the foundations of all departments of knowledge ; in
brief, Pansophia in its elements. He thanks all for
their co-operation, and impresses on them, in eloquent
language, the duty of maintaining the school, and prosecuting the methods which he had taught them, which
he elsewhere sums up in the words, *Noscenda noscendo,
facienda faciendo*, or *Autopsy*, looking at things for oneself, and *Autopraxy*, doing or constant practice.

'Vale Patakina schola!' he concludes. 'Vale ecclesia!
Vale Patakum ipsum ! Valete omnes amici, Comeniique
vestri amicam apud vos retinete memoriam, amicis pro-
sequimini votis, etc. . . . Imprimis valete vos dilecti
collegae, atque si me Eliam vestrum fuisse credebatis et
ob meum a vobis discessum lugetis, ego vos ut meos
Elisaeos intueor et vobis de spiritu meo portionem
duplam coelitus dari opto ; ut publici boni amore et
pro illo promovendo laborum tolerantiâ et ad infirmiores
condescentia progressibus denique bonis ita me superetis
quomodo miraculis patrandis Eliam superavit Elisaeus :
ad scholam hanc vestram et alias tam sancte sapienterque
regendum quam sancte sapienterque scholas Prophet-
arum rexit Elisaeus !'

It must have been about 1652-53, while still in the
midst of his Patak labours, that he lost his best friend
and patron, Ludovic de Geer. A long letter of condo-
lence addressed to the son, Laurence, then settled at
Amsterdam as Swedish ambassador, concludes the third
volume of the Works. In this he recalls the virtues
and lauds the character of the father, who was, without

doubt, a man of high public spirit, and of a generous and liberal nature. For eight years he had supported Comenius and his amanuenses, and was prepared, when the opportunity offered, to contribute largely towards the institution of a Pansophic College.

From Patak Comenius went, in 1654, to his former home at Lesna. The war which almost immediately after broke out (1655) involved the whole of Poland, and caused, among other calamities, the destruction of Lesna (1656).[1] He was thus forced to seek for some safer asylum.

In the overthrow of the town, Comenius lost all his property, including his library and manuscripts, which contained the results of the studies which he had undertaken with a view to the great Pansophic book which was the chief aim of his life. Among the MSS. was one which, he tells us, he considered the most precious of his possessions ; it was his *Silva* or ' forest' (to use his own peculiar expression) of Pansophic materials, a treasury of definitions of all things, and of axioms, scientific and philosophic, which he had spent twenty years in gathering together. He had not, even then, been prepared with a complete system, but he had in contemplation, and nearly ready, a much more complete treatise than any he had yet issued.

After the ruin of Lesna, he was invited by Laurence

---

[1] The fate of Lesna was said to have been partly due to a panegyric on Charles Gustavus, King of Sweden, which Comenius indiscreetly published.

de Geer, the son of his former patron, to join him in Amsterdam, there to take counsel as to his future. From the temporary refuge which he had found for his family he was driven by pestilence, and other friends joining De Geer in urging him to make Amsterdam his future home, he yielded, because, he himself says, 'I have all my life long been accustomed to yield to what seemed to be the guidance of Providence.'[1] Comenius was now sixty-three years of age.

To the loss of his Pansophic MSS. were now added fresh demands on his time of a strictly scholastic kind, and he had to return 'ad puerilia illa utut mihi toties nauseata Latinitatis studia.' An edition of his *Schola Ludus* was demanded in Holland, and he found so many errors and defects in the version printed at Patak after his departure, that he had to devote a considerable time to emending and printing. Then, it was impossible to escape from the supposed necessity of constructing another elementary book, a sequel to the *Vestibulum,*— to be entitled the *Auctarium.* He was also requested by the Senate of Amsterdam to try his method on two youths. His Latinity also was attacked, and this caused him to write *Pro Latinitate Januae Comenianae Apologia.* These labours, but especially this last treatise, revived an interest in his method in the minds of many public men, and he was asked to put his educational views in the form of an epitome, so that busy men might read them. This gave rise to his *Synopsis Novissimae*

---

[1] The last Dedicatory Epistle.

Methodi, which, however, he did not think it worth his while to republish in his Works, probably because it is substantially repeated in other treatises.

The publication of his complete didactic works, to which he now addressed himself at the instance of De Geer, and under the patronage of the highest authorities in Amsterdam, led him to take a critical survey of all he had written, that he might confirm, retract, or modify the opinions which he had from time to time given forth. This treatise of retrospect and revision he entitled *Ventilabrum Sapientiae sive sapienter sua retractandi Ars*—'The Fanner of Wisdom, or the Art of retracting one's own Opinions.' This fanner was to winnow away the chaff and leave the solid grain. He quotes Philo in support of this self-criticism: 'Scientiae finis non contingit hominibus. Nemo enim absolutus est in ulla scientia. Revera perfectiones et vestigia unius sunt (*nempe Dei*).' He also quotes Aristotle as saying, 'It behoves a philosopher to forswear even his own dogmas,' and a Roman Pontiff as remarking, 'Wretched is that man who is the slave of his own dogmas.'

In the *Didactica Magna*, which contains the systematic development of his principles and methods, he finds that he has nothing to retract, but confines himself to a defence of the Syncretic Method, which is there followed. Comenius recognises three methods of ascertaining and expounding truth,—the Analytic and the Synthetic (which words he uses in our modern acceptation), and the Syncretic. By this last he means arguing by a method of parallels in nature,—the method of Analogy. He holds that the true character and process of anything in the created world furnishes a line of explanation for other things, which is of the most convincing kind. The stricter view of Analogy which is now accepted was not known to Comenius, although he must have had before him the dictum of the schoolmen: 'Similia illustrant quidem, non autem probant.'

When, in the course of his retrospect, he re-peruses his *Praeludium Pansophicum*, a sense of wasted years oppresses him, and he is again afflicted with grief, because he had, at the urgent entreaty of friends, too readily deserted this the main line of his studies, sacrificing the great ambition of his life to occupy himself exclusively with matters didactic. 'How badly have I imitated,' he exclaims, 'that merchant seeking for good pearls, who, when he had found a pearl of great price, went away and sold all he had, and bought it! Oh wretched sons of light, who know not to imitate the wisdom of the children of the world! Would that I, having once struck the Pansophic vein, had followed it up, neglecting all else! But so it happens when we lend an ear to the solicitations clamouring outside us rather than to the light shining within us.'

The corrections he has to make on his various didactic writings are certainly very unimportant. They all point in the direction of greater simplification, and for this he looks to the labours of his successors rather than to any revision of his own.

About the year 1657 Comenius wrote and published
(in the fourth volume of his Works) four treatises, which
however constitute one.   He desired to present his
principles in a brief and condensed, yet systematic way,
so that they might be accessible to men occupied with
public affairs.   The first of these treatises is entitled *E
Scholasticis Labyrinthis Exitus in Planum, sive Machina
Didactica mechanice constructa: ad non haerendum amplius (in Docendi et Discendi muniis) sed progrediendum*,
'An Issue out of School-labyrinths into the Open, or
a Didactic Machine mechanically constructed with a
view to no longer sticking fast in the work of Teaching and Learning, but of advancing in them.'   Schools,
he tells us, are to be compared to labyrinths, infinitely
distracting the minds of youth: the thread which is to
guide us through the labyrinths is a true and simple
method.   The sciences and arts and tongues are to be
taught, but the precise quantity and goal of teaching
are not accurately laid down.   The thread of Ariadne—
Method—is all-important, because it leads to distinct
issues by a proper way.   Augustine says, *Praestet pauca
scire quam infinita opinari;* Pliny says, *Satius sit minus
serere et melius arare;* and again, Seneca, *Melius est
scire pauca et iis recte uti quam scire multa quorum
ignores usum.*   'Our method,' says Comenius, 'offers few
things, but these necessary to life here and hereafter;
few things, but these well consolidated by continued
exercises; few things, but these having a direct utility.'

As he grew older, and looked back on his past work,

he became more and more convinced that he was
right in his aims and methods. He was now sixty-five
years of age. His views assumed to his mind a
definite and clear shape, and became almost axiomatic.
He admits certain errors in the details of working out
his views; for example, that his text-books are too
condensed, and attempt too much, and that it would
be hardly possible to accomplish in three years (the
Three-Class philological, or Latin school) all that he
once thought might be accomplished within that
period; but these faults he considers to be faults of
detail, and due to his own culpable neglect of the
principles he had himself laid down. Admitting so
much, he yet regards his method as so absolute in
its character that it may be likened to a machine—
a clock, or a ship, or a mill. Set it going, and keep it
going, and you will find the result certain. It is really
of the nature of a mechanical construction, mechanically constructed. He is never weary of advocating
his system. He sums up his principles, and then, with
all the ardour of his youth, he afresh proceeds to consider the means by which his great end is to be attained.

The Latin school is to be a college in which nothing
but Latin is to be spoken. *Longum et difficile iter per
praecepta, usu et consuetudine iter breve et efficax.* He
calls the brief treatise in which he advocates the institution of such a college *Latium Redivivum*, and urges
the authorities of Amsterdam to institute one.

With such a College he sees his way so to carry out
his methods as to justify him in recurring to one of his

old ideas, and comparing his method to a printing-press, which makes the impression of the type on the paper without fail. So will the impression on minds by his method be equally certain. Hence the name of his next paper, *Typographeum Vivum*, or the Living Printing Press. He here compares his method with clocks, ships, agriculture (*Ingenium enim vivus ager est; Disciplinae aratro sementi praeparandus, Doctrinarum seminibus obserendus, Exercitiorum pluvia, sole, vento animandus*), with the pictorial and sculptural arts, and with architecture, but prefers to dwell on its likeness to the typographic art, not only as to the mode of procedure, but also the result; for whereas in the one case you have books, in the other, every capable pupil properly trained will be a walking library—*obambulans Bibliotheca*.

But the final aim of all this training is moral and religious. Comenius never lost sight of this. As the restoration of man to the Paradise which he forfeited, and to the image of God which he lost, is the aim of the Providence of God in Christ, so the aim of the school is a restoration—a bringing of its work and methods into a harmony with moral and religious aims, and subordinating the school to the Church as a spiritual society. Hence the title of the next treatise, *Paradisus Juventuti Christianae reducendus*. In this treatise he mixes up the spiritual aim of the school with that of a Paradise in the sense of a place that may be made a happy one for boys, and indulges also in many forced analogies between the school and the first Paradise.

Finally, in his *Traditio Lampadis* he solemnly hands over the didactic work of his life to be carried on by others, and commends his labours to God, who had so favoured him as to make him the instrument of sowing the seed of a better time for schools, and to whose blessing he looks for a rich harvest in the future.

Comenius was now sixty-six years of age, and had just revised and completed the issue of his collected Didactic works, extending to four folio volumes. He had now said his last word. We can well believe the simple-hearted and single-minded old Bishop, when he tells us that he had been led by no personal ambition to publish his works, and that he was very far from desiring to derogate from the claims of those writers who preceded him, and to whom he acknowledges his obligations. Nor had his motive been the desire of wealth, for he had sought nothing and gained nothing. He had laboured and written, he says, influenced by the love of God, and stimulated by the exhortations of learned men, solely in the hope of improving the education of youth, and preparing a better future for humanity.

It is not to be supposed that Comenius's relations to his original patron Ludovic de Geer were always pleasant; such relations seldom are. De Geer complained of unnecessary delay, and Comenius had many personal vexations to contend with arising out of his pecuniary dependence. We learn also, from the last

Dedicatory Epistle written by Comenius, and addressed to some of the leading men in Amsterdam, that he had not, even in his old age, escaped the general fate of reformers. While his views on Education had been ardently supported by some of the best men in Europe, that obstructive of all education known as the 'practical teacher,' who is almost always an obscurantist, had been at work. Detraction was busy, and he was accused by the teachers of Amsterdam of 'attacking schools.' To all this his reply was brief. 'I can affirm,' he writes, 'from the bottom of my heart, that these forty years my aim has been simple and un-pretending, indifferent whether I teach or be taught, admonish or be admonished, willing to act the part of a teacher of teachers, if in anything it may be permitted me to be so, and a disciple of disciples where progress may be possible. They say that I write *against* schools: nay, it is *for* schools that I speak, and have spoken. I presume our common ends are the same ; it is as to methods and ways that we differ.' Malignity even touched the character and motives of the old Bishop. ' I have not, by the grace of God,' he says, 'so spent my life that now in my old age I must avoid the light ; nor are the things I have done till now of so little account that I am to keep silence when I am asked to speak. As to the allegation that I have preferred private to public schools, this is incorrect ; my writings show this. I have desired to give trouble to none, but rather to lessen trouble. Why then should any delight to molest me ? Let me live in tranquillity as long as God wills me to be here ! With Thomas à Kempis

I can from my heart and the bitter lessons of experience say, "I have tried all things, nor anywhere have
I found peace, save in a little corner and a little book"
(*angululo et libellulo*).[1]

Of Comenius's domestic life and history not very
much is known. He married, as his second wife, the
daughter of Joh. Cyrillus, a priest of the Brotherhood
and a Senior, apparently about the year 1629. She
died in 1648, or the beginning of 1649, after having
borne five children—a son, Daniel by name, and four
daughters. The eldest daughter, Dorothea, seems to
have married Johann Mohtor, a man of good Slovack
family, who had been under Comenius's educational
supervision at Lissa. The second daughter, Elizabeth,
married Figulus, one of her father's *collaborateurs*, and a
Moravian pastor.

Comenius continued to reside in Amsterdam, after
the publication of his collected Didactic works (completed in the end of 1657), maintaining himself and his
family by teaching, and partly, it would seem, supported
by the private liberality of the admirers of his life and
labours—especially the De Geer family, at whose
expense his books were printed. He dedicated his
works to the city of Amsterdam, in gratitude for the
hospitality its people had shown to him. He lived for
nearly thirteen years after this, dying on the 15th of

---

[1] The attack on Comenius by Nicolas Arnoldus, in his *Discursus
Theologicus contra Comenium*, is personal and spiteful. Bayle's
treatment of Comenius shows a complete misapprehension of his
character.

November 1671, in his eightieth year, and was buried at Naarden. During these concluding years he does not seem to have added to his Didactic writings, but he printed several treatises of a religious character intended to further the promotion of the unity of Protestant Christendom, and continued to maintain by correspondence his connection with the Moravian Brethren, and the superintendence of their affairs. His last publication was a confession, entitled *One Thing Needful*,[1] in which the piety of his heart and the simplicity of his faith are alike conspicuous. In this he thanks God that he had been a man of aspirations.

Even in the declining years of his laborious life he never for a moment lost sight of his great Pansophic work, which was to place before the world of science and letters the sum of human knowledge in all departments, and was to be a University of scientific investigation. He set himself diligently to replace the materials and MSS. which were destroyed at the sacking of Lesna, and left a large number of papers behind him, enjoining his son Daniel and his old friend and fellow-worker Nigrinus to prepare them for publication. The son seems to have troubled himself very little about the matter, but Nigrinus worked for eight or nine years at the revision

---

[1] Unum necessarium in vita et morte et post mortem quod non-necessarii mundi fatigatus et ad unum necessarium sese recipiens senex J. A. Comenius anno aetatis suae 77, mundo expendendum offert. Terent. *Ad omnia aetate sapimus recte.* Edit. Amstelodami 1668. Afterwards republished in Leipzig in 1734.

A translation of the Bible into Turkish also occupied much of his thoughts and time.

and preparation of the MS., being supported during the task by the liberality of Gerard de Geer. But it does not appear that any Pansophic publication ever saw the light.

'Comenius,' says Von Raumer truly, 'is a grand and venerable figure of sorrow. ,Wandering, persecuted, and homeless, during the terrible and desolating Thirty Years' War, he yet never despaired ; but with enduring truth, and strong in faith, he laboured unweariedly to prepare youth by a better education for a better future. Suspended from the ministry, as he himself tells us, and an exile, he had become an Apostle *ad gentes minutulas—Christianam juventutem ;* and certainly he laboured for them with a zeal and love worthy of the chief of the Apostles.'

WORKS OF COMENIUS.

Comenius wrote various books on Physics and a great many on Theological and Ecclesiastical subjects, in addition to those on Education and on Pansophy. The chief of these were :—

1. The Labyrinth of the World and the Paradise of the Heart. Printed in the Czech language about 1621, but first published at Lesna, in quarto, in 1631.

2. Historia unitatis fratrum et ratio disciplinae.

3. Physicae ad Lumen Divinum reformatae Synopsis. Lipsiae 1633, and Amsterodami 1643.

4. De bono Unitatis et Ordinis, Disciplinae et Obedientiae in Ecclesia rectè constituta, vel constituenda : Ecclesiae Bohemicae ad Anglicanam Paraenesis. Amst. 1660.

5. Lux in tenebris (a book on the fulfilment of prophecy in modern events). 1650.

6. Historia Revelationum.
7. Unum Necessarium. Amst. 1668.[1]

EDUCATIONAL AND PANSOPHIC WORKS.

These were published at Amsterdam in 1657, in four vols. folio. They are bound in one volume, and extend to 2271 pages.[2]

·In the Dedicatory Epistle, dated 20th December 1657, the author informs us that he had collected all his writings, arranging them in chronological order, at the request of many leading men in the State, and in compliance with a resolution of the governing body (*sacri senatus decreto*). He dedicates his works to the city of Amsterdam in recognition of the hospitable reception it had given him.

The title is :—

J. A. Comenii Opera didactica omnia, variis hucusque occasioni- bus scripta, diversisque locis edita : nunc autem non tantum in unum, ut simul sint, collecta, sed et ultimo conatu in Systema unum mechanice constructum, redacta. Amsterodami impensis D. Laurentii de Geer excuderunt Christophorus Cunradus et Gabriel a Roy. Anno 1657. 4 voll. fol.

Erster Theil. (Schriften von 1627-1642.) *The Poland Period.*

1. De primis occasionibus, quibus huc studiorum delatus fuit Author, brevissima relatio.
2. Didactica magna. Omnes omnia docendi artificia exhibens.
3. Schola materni gremii, sive de provida Juventutis primo sexennio Educatione.
4. Scholae vernaculae delineatio.
- 5. Janua latinae linguae primum edita.
6. Vestibulum ei praestructum.
7. Proplasma Templi Latinitatis Dav. Vechneri : et cur opus non processerit.
8. De sermonis Latini studio.

---

[1] Also, a History of the Persecutions of the Moravians, the precise title of which I do not know.

[2] The paging 451 to 591, vol. iii., is repeated by the printer.

9. Prodromus pansophiae.
10. Variorum de eo Censurae.
11. Pansophicorum Conatuum Dilucidatio.

Zweiter Theil. (Schriften von 1642-50.) *The Elbing Period.*

1. De novis Didactica studia continuandi occasionibus.
2. Methodus linguarum novissima fundamentis didacticis, solide superstructa.
3. Lat. linguae Vestibulum, rerum et linguae cardines exhibens.
4. Januae linguarum novissimae Clavis, Grammatica Latino-vernacula.
5. Judicia novaeque disquisitiones.

Dritter Theil. (Schriften von 1650-54.) *The Patak Period.*

1. De vocatione in Hungariam relatio.
2. Scholae pansophicae delineatio.
3. De repertis studii pansophici obicibus.
4. De ingeniorum cultura.
5. De ingenia colendi primario instrumento, Libris.
6. De reperta ad Authores latinos prompte legendos et intelligendos facili, brevi et amoena via Schola Triclassi.
7. Eruditionis scholasticae pars I. Vestibulum, rerum et linguae fundamenta ponens.
8. Eruditionis scholasticae pars II. Janua rerum linguarum structuram externam exhibens; embracing
   a. Lexicon Januale.
   b. Grammatica Janualis.
   c. Janualis rerum et verborum contextus, historiolam rerum continens.
9. Eruditionis scholasticae pars III. Atrium rerum et linguarum ornamenta exhibens.
10. Fortius redivivus, sive de pellenda Scholis ignavia.
11. Praecepta morum in usum Juventutis collecta. Anno 1653.
12. Leges bene ordinatae scholae.
13. Orbis sensualium pictus. (Only an announcement.)
14. Schola Ludus: h. e. Januae linguarum praxis comica.
15. Laborum scholasticorum in Hungaria obitorum Coronis.

Vierter Theil. (Schriften von 1654-57.) *The Amsterdam Period.*

1. Vita gyrus, sive de occasionibus vitae, et quibus Autorem in Belgium deferri, iterumque ad intermissa didactica studia redire contigit.

2. Parvulis parvulus, Omnibus omnia, h. e. Vestibuli Latinae linguae Auctarium, voces primitivas in sententiolas redigens.

3. Apologia pro Latinitate Januae Comenianae.

4. Ventilabrum sapientiae, sive sapienter sua retractandi ars.

5. E labyrinthis scholasticis exitus tandem in planum, sive Machina didactica mechanice constructa.

6. Latium redivivum, hoc est, de forma latinissimi Collegii, seu novae romanae civitatulae ; ubi latina lingua usu et consuetudine ut olim, melius tamen quam olim, addiscatur.

7. Typographeum vivum, hoc est : ars compendiose et tamen copiose ac eleganter sapientiam non chartis, sed ingeniis imprimendi.

8. Paradisus ecclesiae reductus ; hoc est optimus scholarum status, ad primae paradisiacae scholae ideam delineatus.

9. Traditio lampadis, hoc est studiorum sapientiae christianaeque juventutis et scholarum, Deo et hominibus devota commendatio.

10. Paralipomena didactica.

———

Pansophiae diatyposis. Dantzic 1643.

In 1670 Comenius, when (as he states) he was seventy-eight years of age, wrote a short preface to a trilingual edition of the *Janua*—English, Latin, and Greek, in parallel columns—published in London. Some quaint woodcuts of by no means bad execution are prefixed to this edition, which I met with in the Advocates' Library, Edinburgh. The cuts are illustrative of the different departments of realistic study, as then understood. In these we have represented Astronomy, Mathematics, Navigation, Geography, Anatomy, Architecture. One of the anatomical illustrations is a skeleton leaning in a pensive attitude on a table, while one long bony hand rests on a skull.

THE EDUCATIONAL SYSTEM AND
WRITINGS OF COMENIUS.

PART I.

THE GREAT DIDACTIC.

First Section.

PANSOPHY AND THE AIM OF EDUCATION.

THERE can be no doubt that it was chiefly the specu-
lations of Lord Verulam that fired the imagination of
Comenius, and led him to conceive hopes of reducing
all existing learning to a systematic form, and providing
for all the more ambitious youth of Europe, in a great
Pansophic College, opportunities for the universal study
of the whole body of science. To this universal and
systematised learning he gave the name of Pansophia
or Encyclopædia. He was filled with high hopes of the
benefits which would arise from a revision and arrangement of human knowledge—hopes which he shared
with many men of his time, and which it would be
rash for us to say were without sufficient foundation.

The title of one of his treatises is 'A Prelude of
Pansophy, in which the necessity of universal wisdom,
its possibility and its practicability (if it be approached
according to a certain method) is briefly and clearly
demonstrated.' He draws a picture of the confusion

of existing knowledge, and the inadequacy of the treatment of its various departments. He attributes this to the ignorance of those in one place of what had been done elsewhere, and to the too great specialisation of inquirers. The writer on jurisprudence was ignorant, it might be, of philosophy and physics, the writer on physics was ignorant of metaphysics, the writer on metaphysics and ethics ignored physics; and so forth. Hence inadequacy of treatment; hence, too, the fragmentary presentation of all knowledge. To cure this it was necessary that there should be an authorised and systematised view of all learning arranged in a philosophic order. Men who, in the higher departments of education, had been disciplined in this encyclopædia, would have an universal culture that would enable them to prosecute special branches with greater firmness and accuracy. He called on learned men to enable him by their contributions to construct such a book, or series of books. As to method; while the spirit of the Baconian induction was in him, in so far as he based knowledge on observation and on advancing from particulars to generals, he had not grasped induction in its true significance. For, as Bacon himself points out, the senses by themselves are not to be trusted, and the processes of a true investigation are to supplement, correct, and verify them.

As all knowledge was to lead to God, and to God as revealed through Christ, Comenius spoke of his encyclopædism as a Christian Pansophy, and called the various sections 'the seven parts of the temple of Christian Pansophy.' The first part was to show the necessity and possibility of the temple and to give its external structure or outline—to be called the *Templi Sapientiae Propylaeum.* The second part was to give the first approach to a knowledge of all knowable things—a general apparatus of wisdom—in which the highest genera and fundamental principles and axioms were to be exhibited, from which, as the primal sources of truth, the streams of all sciences flow and diverge,—to be called the *Porta.* The third part (the *primum Atrium*) was to exhaust visible nature. The fourth (the *Atrium medium*) was to treat of man and reason; the fifth part (*Atrium internum*), of man's essential nature—free-will and responsibility, and the repair of man's will in Christ as the beginning of the spiritual life. The sixth part (*Sanctum sanctorum*) was to be theological, and here man was to be admitted to the study and worship of God and his revelation, that thereby he might be led to embrace God as the centre of eternal life. The seventh part (*Fons aquarum viventium*) was to expound the use of true wisdom and its dissemination, so that the whole world might be filled with a knowledge of God.

This is a sketch of a Pansophic scheme of knowledge and of a corresponding Pansophic University. The same ideas worked out as applicable to a Secondary or Latin School will be found in the sequel under the designation, 'The Inner Organisation of a Pansophic School.'

Comenius was a thoroughgoing Realist in education, but he combined with this a fervent evangelicalism: indeed, his whole purpose was to lead youth to God through *things*—to God as the source of all, and as the crown of knowledge and the end of life.

I have chosen to introduce the educational reader

to Comenius in connection with his Pansophic schemes, because they are the key to his intellectual life and his educational aims. For it will be seen in the sequel that the idea of a Christian Pansophy never deserts him, and that, from his 'mother-school' upwards, his purpose is to give to children and boys the elements of universal knowledge adapted to the various stages of school life. It is as the representative of encyclopædism in education (in his case a Christian encyclopædism), and as the first exhaustive writer on general method, that Comenius claims our attention. As a type of the realistic and encyclopædic school of Educationalists, he will probably never be superseded.

I shall now give an account of those works of Comenius in which he endeavoured to give effect to his Pansophic educational views and his methods.

The 'Great Didactic'[1] (*Magna Didactica*) first arrests

[1] The word is of singular number, and *Ars* is understood. The full title of the book is as follows :—

DIDACTICA MAGNA ;
UNIVERSALE OMNES OMNIA
DOCENDI ARTIFICIUM EXHIBENS :
Sive certus et exquisitus modus, per omnes alicujus Christiani Regni communitates, Oppida et Vicos, tales erigendi Scholas, ut Omnis utriusque sexus Juventus, nemine usquam neglecto, Literis informari, Moribus expoliri, Pietate imbui, eaque ratione intra pubertatis annos ad omnia quae praesentis et futurae vitae sunt instrui possit,
Compendiosè, Jucundè, Solidè :
Ubi omnium quae suadentur,
Fundamenta, ex ipsissima rerum natura eruuntur :
Veritas, artium Mechanicarum, parallelis exemplis demonstratur :
Series, per Annos, Menses, Dies, Horas, disponitur ;
Via denique in effectum haec feliciter
deducendi, facilis et certa ostenditur.

our attention, because it was put forth as a systematic treatment of the whole question of Education. Here our object will be to make Comenius speak as much as possible for himself.

In his prefatory remarks to the Great Didactic, Comenius tells us that the Didactic Art has to be studied in the interests of Parents, Teachers, Pupils, the Commonwealth, the Church, and Heaven.

'Quidnam,' says Diogenes the Pythagorean, 'est fundamentum totius reipublicae? Adolescentium educatio. Haud enim unquam vites utilem fructum protulerint quae non bene sunt excultae.' ' It is our bounden duty,' he adds, 'to consider the means whereby the whole body of Christian youth may be stirred to vigour of mind and the love of Heavenly things.'

General Statement of Aim.

I. Man is the last, the most complete, and the most excellent of living creatures.

II. The final end of man lies beyond this life. This life is threefold, viz., Vegetative, Animal, and Intellectual or Spiritual. The first nowhere manifests itself outside the body; the second stretches forth to objects through the operations of the senses; the third is able to exist separately as well as in the body, as in the case of Angels. 'Jam quia evidens est, supremum hunc vitae gradum a prioribus valide in nobis obumbrari et praepediri, necessario sequitur futurum esse ubi in ἀκμὴν deducatur.'

III. This life is only a preparation for an eternal life. The visible world is· a seed-plot, a boarding-house and training-school for man.

'As certainly as the period spent in the mother's womb is a preparation for the life in the body, so certainly is the dwelling in the body a preparation for that life which will take up the present and endure for ever. Happy he who has brought forth from his mother's womb well-formed limbs : happier a thousand times he who carries *hence* a well-formed soul.'

IV. There are three steps of preparation for Eternity. 'Se, et secum omnia, nôsse; Regere; et ad Deum Dirigere.'

It is accordingly required of man that—

(1.) He should know all things.

(2.) He should have power over all things and over himself.

(3.) He should refer himself and all things to God, the Source of All.

These requirements are summed up in the words *Eruditio, Virtus seu Mores Honesti, Religio seu Pietas,* —Knowledge, Virtue, and Piety. All else is merely accidental and extrinsic.

V. The seeds of these three (Knowledge, Virtue, and Religion) are in us by Nature, *i.e.* our first original and fundamental nature, to which we are to be recalled by God in Christ.

It is as certain that Men has been born fit for the understanding of things, the harmony of morals, and the love of God, as that there are roots to a tree.

KNOWLEDGE, or *Eruditio.*—God has placed the roots of eternal wisdom in man. · He is fit to acquire all knowledge, because he is the image of God. God is omniscient, and the mind of man is like a polished globular mirror hung up in a chamber, which receives the forms (species) of all things. The body, the voice, the vision of man are limited, but the mind is unlimited in its sweep—it is capable of all things.

Again, Man is a microcosm in which are enfolded the seeds of all *things*, as well as of all knowledge. To him, as inhabiting a natural body, are attached emissaries and scouts, viz., his senses of seeing, hearing, smelling, taste, and touch.

There is implanted in man a desire to know, and not merely a tolerance of labour, but an appetite for labour. The senses, *e.g.*, *seek about* for objects.

The mind may be compared to the earth, for does it not receive all kinds of seeds? or, as Aristotle said, to a *tabula rasa*, on which nothing is inscribed, but on which everything *may be* inscribed; or the brain may be compared to wax, on which every form may be imprinted; for which the wisdom of God is to be admired, who has made it, though small, capable of receiving innumerable impressions.

Most fitly perhaps, is the mind to be compared to a mirror, which reflects accurately all that is placed before it.

VIRTUE, or *Mores Honesti.*—The seeds of moral life are connate with man. He is adapted for a *harmonia morum*. In the motions of the soul the principal wheel is the will. The weights which drive this wheel are the affections and appetites, but the reason is as a movable bolt which opens and shuts the entrance of these, and suspends or directs.

PIETY, or *Religio.*—So also are the roots of religion in man, for is he not the image of God? The soul of man longs after its likeness. God is the end of its striving, and this is the *summum bonum*—a longing not wholly extinguished by the Fall. We are not to forget our restoration in the new Adam. Everything returns willingly to its own true nature, and it is easier for man, by the grace of the Holy Spirit, to be wise, good, and holy than it is for his adventitious depravity to stop his progress.

Nature gives the *seeds* of knowledge, morality, and religion, but it does not give knowledge, virtue, and religion themselves. These have to be striven for. Hence man is truly called *animal disciplinabile*, since he cannot truly become a man except through discipline. Man, then, has to be educated to become a man. Even to use his limbs aright, he has to be educated. The mind, if weak or stupid, we all admit, needs discipline; but this is true even of the capable understanding; for as rich soil, if not rightly tilled, grows weeds and thistles in more than usual abundance, so is it with the man of natural talent.

Education is to be carried out while the mind is yet tender and the brain soft. And in order that the human being may be educated to full humanity, God has given him certain years of childhood during which he is not fit for active life ; and that only is firm and stable which has been imbibed during the earliest years.

The care of children belongs properly to their parents, but they need the help of those specially set apart for education—*preceptores, ludimagistri, professores*—and there is, consequently, a need for schools and colleges. Schools should be instituted in every part of the empire, and the whole of the youth of both sexes should be sent to these. Schools have been truly called *humanitatis officinae* (workshops or manufactories of Humanity), where man may be trained to be — 1. A rational creature ; 2. A creature lord of other creatures and of himself; 3. A creature which shall be the joy of his Creator.

That only I call a school, Comenius says, which is truly *officina hominum*, where minds are instructed in wisdom to penetrate all things, where souls and their affections are guided to the universal harmony of the virtues, and hearts are allured to divine love,—'ubi omnes omnia omnino doceantur.'

Luther, in 1525, in his exhortation to the States of the Empire to erect schools, desires, *inter alia*, these two things—'(1) That in all cities, towns, and villages schools be instituted to teach all the youth of both sexes ; so that those engaged in agriculture and trades might receive two hours' daily instruction in letters, morals, and religion. (2) That they should be instructed according to some easier method, which would not only not deter from study, but allure to it, so that they should derive no less pleasure from their studies than from their games.' But even now, 'ubi universales illae scholae? ubi blanda illa methodus?' Even those that exist for the wealthier classes are a terror to boys and torture-chambers of minds. As to moral training and manners, even the Universities are bad. And why all this? Because 'de bene vivendo in scholis quaestio nulla movetur.' They have sought only knowledge, not morality and religion.

And how have they sought this? In such a way that they spend five, ten, or even more years over what could be done in one year. What is capable of being instilled and poured into the mind in the gentlest way is violently stuffed in and stamped in. What might be placed perspicuously and clearly before the eyes is presented in an obscure, perplexed, and intricate way.

The mind is nowhere nourished with the true kernel of things, but with the mere husk of words.

As to the study of the Latin tongue—good Heavens! how laborious, how intricate, how prolix! Mere scullions, cooks, and soldiers will learn one, two, or three foreign tongues more quickly than the pupils of our schools will learn Latin only; and these know little of it, and are dependent on their lexicons. This *must* arise from a bad method. Well may the distinguished Lubinus say that, when he thinks of the immense labour, tedium, and loss in the teaching of Latin, he is disposed to think that the method must have been invented by some evil genius—an enemy of the human race. But why multiply testimony? I myself am an unhappy instance of wasted boyhood and youth—years misspent, the memory of which I recall with tears and sighs. But the past is irrevocable. Let us do better for our posterity.

So much for the general Aim of Education according to Comenius. He now proceeds to treat of Method, taking the operations of external nature as his guide. The parallelism is throughout forced, and often fanciful.

————

METHOD.

THE METHOD OF EDUCATION.

REFORMATION is possible. I undertake an organisation of schools whereby—

(1.) All the youth may be instructed save those to whom God has denied intelligence.

(2.) And instructed in all those things which make a man wise, good, and holy.

(3.) And *that*, as a preparation for life, in such a time as will set him free before he is adult.

(4.) And *that*, without blows, severity, or compulsion, but most lightly, gently, and, so to speak, spontaneously.

(5.) And *that*, in such a way that they shall be trained, not to specious and superficial, but to true and solid learning, and to the use of their own faculties. —not to dependence on others or on mere memory. With like solidity will they be instructed in morality and religion.

(6.) And *that*, so that the course of instruction shall not be laborious, but very easy; four hours a day being sufficient.

Order it is that is the soul of the world; order sustains nature in all its parts.

Order too is the eye of the school, and we must take from nature the order of the school.

Our business is to discover from the indications of nature the principles which underlie the answers to the following queries :—

(1.) How life may be so prolonged as to enable us to learn all things.

(2.) How arts may be shortened with a view to rapid learning.

(3.) How we may seize the right occasions for learning so as to learn *Surely*.

(4.) How we may unlock the mind so as to learn *Easily*.

(5.) How we may sharpen the understanding so as to learn *Solidly*.

Omitting other points, let us consider the three problems contained in the words *surely, easily, solidly*—

CERTÓ, FACILÉ, SOLIDÉ.

Certó, or *Surely*.

I. CERTO, *or* SURELY.

How are we to teach and learn surely, i.e. *so as to be sure of our result?*

This is to be done by finding the *modus operandi* of Nature, and accommodating ourselves to that, as follows :[1]—

FIRST PRINCIPLE.—*Nature attends to a fit time.*

Birds do not begin the work of multiplying their species in winter.   So with other natural operations, such as·the growth in a garden; the season determines all.   Right in the teeth of this, schools do not choose a fit time for exercising the minds of pupils; and they do not so accurately arrange the exercises as to insure that all things advance infallibly through their own successive steps.

Just as Nature chooses spring as the time of preparation for future products, so the right time is boyhood— the spring of life.   The right time of the day is the morning hours, which is the spring of the day; and as to arrangement of studies, it may be said, generally, that nothing should be taught except when it can be comprehended.

SECOND PRINCIPLE.—*Nature prepares material for itself before it gives it form.*

In the school-books, matter does not precede form.

---

[1] It will be noticed that successive principles yield the same or similar rules.   Hence considerable repetition.

In schools also they teach words before things—the mere clothing or husk of words before the reality itself. Then in the study of a language they teach form before things, because they teach rules before words and sentences. They give rules and then examples, whereas the light ought to precede that which it is intended to light up.

In all instruction it is necessary that, having got ready the necessary books and materials: (1.) The understanding be instructed before speech is demanded; (2.) That no language should be learned from a Grammar, but from suitable authors, that real studies should precede organic (formal), and that examples should come before rules.

THIRD PRINCIPLE.—*Nature takes a fit subject for its operation, or at least takes care that it be made fit.*

Wherefore—

(1.) Let him who goes to school remain steadily there.

(2.) Whatever study is taken up for treatment, let the minds of the pupils be predisposed towards it (and prepared for it).

(3.) Let all obstacles be removed out of the path of the pupils.

FOURTH PRINCIPLE.—*Nature does not confuse itself in its works, but advances distinctly to one thing after another.*

Wherefore let pupils be occupied with only one

study at a time; that is to say, teach only one thing at a time.

FIFTH PRINCIPLE.—*Nature begins all its operations from within outwards,* e.g. *a tree grows from within,* etc.

Teachers err herein, that instead of diligently explaining and articulating everything, they would acquit themselves of their task of instructing youth, by speaking, dictating, and exercising memory.

Wherefore—

(1.) Let the understanding of things be first formed, then the memory exercised on what is understood, and only in the third place, speech and hand (*i.e.* writing).

(2.) The teacher should attend to every way of opening the intelligence, and must apply them fitly.

SIXTH PRINCIPLE.—*Nature begins all its formation from generals, and thence proceeds to specialise—e.g.* it warms and nourishes the whole mass of the egg, and does not form first the head, then the wings, then thè feet, but, having warmed the whole, it sends its creative force into the special parts, and there specialises. So, a painter in painting a portrait does not draw first the nose, then the ears, etc., but outlines the whole man on the canvas roughly with chalk, and then proceeds to fill in. So with instruction, the outline should first be given.

Wherefore—

(1.) From the very beginning of their instruction, the (principles or) essential groundwork of *all* learning should be given.

(2.) Every language, science, or art should first be learned in its simplest rudiments. Thus the idea of the whole, as a whole, will be grasped; then, more fully, rules and examples should be given; thereafter, peculiarities and anomalies; and finally, if necessary, commentaries, etc.

SEVENTH PRINCIPLE.—*Nature does not proceed* per saltum, *but step by step.* The hatching goes on by insensible degrees. So, a man building a house does not begin from the top but from the foundation, and step by step he rears his structure.

Wherefore—

(1.) The whole sphere of studies should be distributed carefully among the successive classes of the school in such a manner that the earlier study always prepares the way for what is to follow, and, as it were, lights the path to it.

(2.) The time at the teacher's disposal should be carefully distributed, so that its own peculiar task may await every year, month, day, hour.

(3.) This distribution of the time should be most closely attended to, so that nothing may be passed over, and nothing put in its wrong order.

EIGHTH PRINCIPLE.—*Nature, when it once begins, does not stop till it has completed its task.*

Wherefore—

(1.) He who is handed over to the school should be retained there until he is ready to come forth an instructed, moral, and religious man.

(2.) The school should be in an undisturbed locality.[1]

(3.) What has been laid down to be done should be strictly carried on on the lines laid down, and no gap permitted.

(4.) No one should be allowed to absent himself on any pretext.

NINTH PRINCIPLE.—*Nature carefully avoids whatever is contrary to its operations or hurtful.*

Wherefore—

(1.) Permit a scholar the use of no books save those which have to do with his own class.

(2.) The books should be so constructed that they may with truth be called channels of Wisdom, Morality, and Piety.

(3.) Dissolute associates in or out of school are not to be tolerated.

II. FACILE, *or* EASILY.

We have exhibited the principles in accordance with which the work can be done with *certainty*. Now we proceed to show that it can also be done easily and pleasantly. This will be the case if we attend to the following ten principles (many of which repeat what has been already laid down).

I. Let the education begin early, before the mind is corrupted.

[1] This belongs rather to the Third Principle.

II. Let it be done with due preparation of the mind.

III. Let it proceed from the more general to the special.

IV. And from the easy to the more difficult.

V. Let no one be weighted with too much to learn.

VI. Let progress be slow everywhere.

VII. Let the intellect be *forced* to nothing save what it spontaneously desires in accordance with its age and with right method.

VIII. Let everything be communicated through the senses,

IX. And turned to present use.

X. Let all things be taught according to one and the same method.

Let us follow the steps of Nature as illustrative of the above principles.

FIRST PRINCIPLE.—*Nature begins from pure elements.*

The egg which is to be hatched is pure. The tender minds we seek to train should be free from distractions and uncorrupted.

Wherefore—

(1.) Let the education of youth begin early.

(2.) Let there be only one preceptor in each subject for each pupil (*i.e.* do not send the child from one master to another in the same subject).

(3.) Before all, let the morals be reduced to harmony under the influence of the preceptor.

SECOND PRINCIPLE.—*Nature predisposes matter so that it shall seek form.*

The bird hatched *desires* to walk and to peck, and finally desires to fly.

Wherefore—

(1.) The *desire* of knowing and learning is to be stirred up in boys in every way. ἐάν ἦς φιλομαθής ἔσῃ πολυμαθής.—(Isoc.)

(2.) Let the *method* of teaching lessen the labour of learning, so that nothing be a stumbling-block to the pupil and deter from perseverance in study.

This ardour to acquire is to be excited by parents, who should evince their respect for schoolmasters and learning ; by teachers, who should be kind, paternal, and ready to commend ; by schools, which should be pleasant rooms, well lighted, clean, and adorned with pictures, etc. ; by the things which the pupils study, which should be so presented as to attract; by the method, which should be the natural method; and by magistrates, who should be present at examinations and distribute rewards.

THIRD PRINCIPLE.—*Nature draws out all things from beginnings, which in their bulk are small, in their virtue strong.*

Note in connection with this—(1.) That every art be summed up in rules, very short, but very exact. (2.) That every rule be conceived in words as brief as they are lucid. (3.) That numerous examples be given with each rule, so that the applications of the rule, however various, may be clear.

FOURTH PRINCIPLE.—*Nature proceeds from the more easy to the more difficult.*

We find Latin rules taught in Latin—the unknown by the equally unknown, and many other faults which will be amended if

(1.) The teacher speak the same vernacular as the boy. (2.) If all explanations of things be given in a *known* tongue. (3.) If every grammar and lexicon be adapted to that tongue (*i.e.* the vernacular) by means of which the new is to be learned. (4.) If the study of the new tongue advance by degrees—the pupil being taught first to understand, then to write, and finally to speak it (which, being extemporaneous, is the most difficult). (5.) If, when Latin words are given with vernacular, the vernacular words, as being best known, always come first. (6.) If the material of study be so arranged that the scholar learns first that which is nearest, then that which is near, then that which is more remote, and finally that which is most remote (*e.g.* do not seek illustrations from theology or politics, but from things at hand and familiar). (7.) If the senses of boys be first exercised, then the memory, then the intelligence,[1] and finally the judgment. For science takes its beginning from the senses, and thence passes into the memory through imagination, then by induction of singulars an understanding of universals is formed, and finally a judgment as to things understood takes effect, giving the certitude of science.

[1] Intelligence should precede memory, but the term is here used of the generalising power.

FIFTH PRINCIPLE.—*Nature does not overweight itself, but is content with few things at a time—e.g.* it does not demand two birds out of one egg.

SIXTH PRINCIPLE.—*Nature does not hurry itself, but proceeds slowly—e.g.* slow is the hatching of the bird.

Wherefore—

(1.) Spend as few hours as possible in public lessons; four being the right number, as many more being left for private study.

(2.) Fatigue the memory as little as possible, only fundamental things being exacted, all else being allowed to flow freely.

(3.) Proportion all things to the capacity, which, according to the progress of years and studies, will grow of itself.

SEVENTH PRINCIPLE.—*Nature pushes nothing forcibly forward, except what, being already inwardly matured, desires to burst forth—e.g.* the bird does not urge its young to fly till their wings are ready.

Let nothing, then, be done against the grain. The want of desire frequently arises from want of previous preparation and explanation.

Wherefore—

(1.) Let nothing be attempted with youth except those things which their age and ability not only admit of but desire.

(2.) Let nothing be prescribed as a memory-task which has not previously been thoroughly understood.

(3.) Let nothing be prescribed to be done till the

form of it and the rule of imitation have been sufficiently pointed out and impressed.

EIGHTH PRINCIPLE.—*Nature assists itself in every possible way—e.g.* there is vital warmth in the egg itself, as well as in the maternal incubator.

Boys must be so far assisted as to understand what is given them to do. The teacher who demands a task without sufficient explanation and preparation is as cruel as a nurse who would put an infant on the ground and tell it to walk. We must bear patiently with weakness.

Wherefore—

(1.) Let no stripes be inflicted on account of studies : (for if the boy does not learn, whose fault is it save the teacher's, who either does not know how to make the pupil docile, or does not care to do it ?).

(2.) Let what the pupils have to learn be so placed before them and explained that they see it as clearly as their own five fingers.

(3.) And in order that everything may be imprinted the more easily, let the senses be applied to the subject as often as possible—*e.g.* let hearing be joined with vision, and the hand with speech. It is not enough to tell to the ears, but the teacher must present to the eyes, that through them the instruction may reach the imagination. Leave nothing until it has been impressed by means of the ear, the eye, the tongue, the hand. Write up on the walls (or draw) the substance of your teaching. Thus the pupils will also acquire the habit of writing down in their note-books.

NINTH PRINCIPLE.—*Nature produces nothing the use of which is not ultimately apparent*—*e.g.* wings and feet are found to be formed for flying and running.

Wherefore—

Let nothing be taught except for manifest use.

TENTH PRINCIPLE.—*Nature does all things uniformly* —*e.g.* one bird is produced in the same way as all other birds.

Wherefore—

(1.) Let there be one and the same method for instructing in all sciences ; one and the same in all arts ; one and the same in all tongues.

(2.) Let there be for all school-exercises the same order and manner of procedure.

(3.) Use the same editions of books throughout.

III. SOLIDE, *or* SOLIDLY.[1]

Few give a solid amount of instruction to scholars. This is a general complaint.

To cure these evils—

I. Let only things likely to be of solid advantage be treated of.

II. All these should be taught without separating any of them from the curriculum.

---

[1] There is in this chapter a good deal of forcing in order to make it run on ten principles like the preceding. It is enough to enumerate the principles without going into all the details.

III. A solid basis should be laid for each.

IV. That basis should be laid deep.

V. Let everything subsequently aimed at rest on these same foundations.

VI. Wherever distinctions are to be made, let these be distinctly and most articulately made.

VII. Let all studies which follow be founded on those that go before.

VIII. Let all things which as a matter of fact cohere be always connected in teaching.

IX. Let everything be arranged according to its true relation to the understanding, the memory, and the speech.

X. Let everything be firmly implanted by continual exercises.

FIRST PRINCIPLE.—*Nature begins nothing that will be useless.*

Wherefore in schools—

(1.) Let nothing be taught which is not of the most solid utility for this life and the next.

(2.) If some things have to be instilled into youth only for the sake of this life, let them be of such a kind as will not hinder the interests of the eternal life, and as will produce solid fruit for this life.

SECOND PRINCIPLE.—*Nature omits nothing likely to be of benefit to the body it is forming.*

Therefore it is that in schools there must be not merely knowledge, but also morals and piety.

THIRD PRINCIPLE.—*Nature does nothing without a foundation or root.*

Wherefore—

(1.) The love of any studies that are begun should be excited in the pupil.

(2.) The idea (*i.e.* outline or sketch) of the subject to be taught—language or art—should first be given before going to particulars. In this way a foundation is laid in the mind of the pupil.

FOURTH PRINCIPLE.—*Nature sends its roots deep.*

The general idea of the subject to be taught must *therefore* be deeply impressed.

FIFTH PRINCIPLE.—*Nature produces everything from a root ; nothing from any other source.*

Wherefore—

(1.) Let all things be deduced from the unchangeable elements of things.

(2.) Let nothing be learned by authority, but by demonstration, sensible or rational.

(3.) Let nothing be taught by the analytic method only, but rather by the synthetic.

SIXTH PRINCIPLE.—*Nature, the more the uses for which it prepares anything, the more articulately does it differentiate it into parts.*

Wherefore—

Let there be no confusion in instruction.

SEVENTH PRINCIPLE.—*Nature, in each of its works, is in perpetual progress, never halts, and never attempts new things, the former things being cast aside, but only continues what has been previously begun, increases it, and perfects it.*

Wherefore—

(1.) Let all studies be so arranged that the subsequent things shall be founded in what has preceded, and be strengthened by them.

(2.) Let everything which is presented to the pupil, and rightly understood, be fixed in the memory.

EIGHTH PRINCIPLE.—*Nature binds together everything by continuous bonds.*

Wherefore—

(1.) Let the studies of the whole life be so arranged that they shall be one encyclopædia, in which there shall be nothing which does not arise out of a common root, nothing not in its proper place.

(2.) Let everything that is taught be so strengthened by reasons that no room shall be left for doubt or forgetfulness. And further, let all things be taught through their causes.

NINTH PRINCIPLE.—*Nature preserves, between root and branches, a true proportion in respect of quantity and quality.*

Wherefore—

(1.) Let everything taught be at once a subject of reflection as to its use, lest anything should be learned to no purpose (*i.e.* the root of knowledge must spread out into the branches of its various applications).

(2.) Let everything that is learned be communicated to others, that nothing may be known to no purpose.

TENTH PRINCIPLE.—*Nature develops and strengthens itself by frequent movement.*

There must therefore in everything be very frequent repetitions and exercises. This is pressed strongly by Comenius for various reasons.

Hence—

The significance of the well-known distich—

> Multa rogare :—rogata tenere : Retenta docere.
> Haec tria discipulum faciunt superare magistrum.

SCHOOL MANAGEMENT IN RELATION TO SURE, SOLID, AND EASY INSTRUCTION.

Comenius next proceeds to give suggestions for *school management.* This was in his case a demand which the reader was entitled to make, because the contemplated course of instruction was encyclopædic, and it accordingly was difficult to see how the work could be done in the ordinary school life. He held that by beginning in due time, by pursuing good methods, and by basing all instruction in language on the Realities of Knowledge, it was possible to carry youth with ease and certainty through a Pansophic curriculum.

The reasons why more rapid progress is not made in schools are, he says, these—(1.) Because there are no fixed goals marking distinctly how far pupils are to be carried in any one year, month, and day. (2.) Because no way is marked out of infallibly reaching these goals. (3.) Because things that are joined together by nature are not taken up as connected, but separately. *E.g.* Boys are employed in learning to read long before they are taught to write. In Latin, again, boys are required to struggle with the accidence and grammar rules, and with mere words without *things.* He then goes on to point out defects as to the inner organisation of schools —the masters, the classes, and the books—in all which animadversions he is undoubtedly right; but as the defects to which he alludes for the most part no longer exist in schools, we may pass at once to the general rules which he lays down.

He maintains that one teacher will suffice for the instruction of any number of boys. It seems to have been the custom to teach boys either individually, or two or three together, in Comenius's time. Comenius was consequently right in maintaining that a considerable number could be taught together in a class. But he places no limit on the number. Our modern experience tells us there is a limit, if the class is to be sufficiently taught. Comenius admits that the teacher of one hundred boys could not personally ascertain whether all did and understood their work; but by arranging them in tens, and putting one of the boys (whose work he had ascertained to be accurate) over each troop of ten, he might check their exercises and report to the master. The troops of ten he calls *Decuriae*, and their captains *Decuriones*.

Then he gives various practical directions for teaching

a large class, most of which are admirable. *E.g.* The teacher must make all attentive to himself, and this

(1.) By always bringing before his pupils something pleasing and profitable.

(2.) By introducing the subject of instruction in such a way as to commend it to them, or by stirring their intelligences into activity by inciting questions regarding it.

(3.) By standing in a place elevated above the class, and requiring all eyes to be fixed on him.

(4.) By aiding attention through the representation of everything to the senses as far as possible.

(5.) By interrupting his instruction by frequent and pertinent questions—*e.g.* Tu aut tu quid modo dixi? etc. etc.

(6.) If the boy who has been asked a question should fail to answer, by leaping to the second, third, tenth, thirtieth, and asking the answer *without repeating the question.*

(7.) By occasionally demanding an answer from any one in the whole class, and thus stirring up rivalry.

(8.) By giving an opportunity to any to ask questions when the lesson is finished.

In the correction of the numerous written exercises which Comenius would give, it would be necessary, of course, to call in the aid of the Decuriones.

Comenius next speaks of the necessity of all boys using the same books and same editions, and the importance of a careful construction of school-books.

He next advocates the necessity of such careful school-order as will insure that the same thing is done by all at the same time.

Then, that all be taught according to the same method.

Next, that few, but select, words be used for the explanation of things.

He next considers how two or three things can be done together :—

(1.) Let words always be conjoined with things. Thereby we shall learn about realities. ' Id agendum est,' says Seneca, *Ep.* ix., ' ut non verbis serviamus sed sensibus.' (2.) Let the exercises of reading and writing be always conjoined. (3.) Let exercises in style be not *mere* exercises in style, but in matter, so that, while they exercise the mind, they also attain some solid result. (4.) Let what is learnt by the pupils be again taught by them. (5.) Let the serious things of life be imitated in a sportive way in school-exercises,—*e.g.* rivalries may be instituted in certain departments of knowledge (collecting of plants, etc.), and the pupils who are most successful dubbed Licentiate or Doctor. Again, they may be dubbed, in connection with other studies, Kings, Councillors, Chancellors, Secretaries, and so forth. (6.) Let everything advance step by step. (7.) To prevent all delay and retardation of progress, drop out whatever is irrelevant or superfluous or too detailed.

The Art of Education.

THE ART OF EDUCATION—*i.e.* THE APPLICATION OF METHOD TO PRACTICE[1].

WE have now given a view of Comenius's Theory of Education, in respect of Aim and of Method. The remaining half of the treatise, though forming a continuation of the parts which precede it, without any indication of a division, is in point of fact the application of the theory of Method to the Praxis, and repetition is unavoidable.

Comenius recognises the labour which his conception of the school and of method demands of the teacher, and desires to show how that labour may be abbreviated and the work made possible. As education was then conducted, the task which Comenius imposed on teachers would certainly have been beyond their powers. Accordingly, he inquires first into the obstructions which so retarded the work of schools, that those who had spent a large part of their lives in them had not even paid their respects to the Arts and Sciences, much less

[1] The division which I have made is not in Comenius, but I think it gives a clearer view of his system.

acquired a knowledge of them. These obstructions are presented as follows, and they are generally merely the negation of the positive rules of method already enforced :—

(1.) There are no fixed goals marking distinctly how far pupils are to be carried in any one year, month, or day.

(2.) No way of infallibly reaching these goals is marked out.

(3.) Things that have a natural connection are not taken up together, but separately—*e.g.* reading without writing, words without things.

(4.) The arts and sciences are treated of in a fragmentary way, and not encyclopædically.

(5.) Different schools have different methods of procedure;—nay, different teachers in the same school follow diverse methods, and even the same teacher will employ different methods in the different subjects which he teaches.

(6.) The prevalence of individual teaching and the want of classification.

(7.) Increase in the number of masters to meet the above objection only increases the confusion.

(8.) Boys are often allowed by their masters to take up what books they please, both in school and out of school, instead of being kept in definite lines with prescribed books. Boys thus get into a state of mental confusion, from which only the more vigorous spirits ever extricate themselves.

In seeking for remedies, Comenius seeks an analogy

in nature, which, though destitute of intrinsic merit, is yet so characteristic of his fanciful mode of procedure that I may give it here.

Take the Sun in the heavens. By the diffusion of his rays he discharges a laborious and infinite function sufficing for all. And how does he work?

(1.) He does not occupy himself with objects one by one—a tree or an animal,—but illumines and warms the whole earth.

(2.) By the *same* rays he lights up all, and discharges himself of all his functions.

(3.) At the same time through all regions he gives rise to spring and summer, autumn and winter.

(4.) He preserves the same order of operation ; as he is to-day, so to-morrow,—as he is this year, so next.

(5.) He produces everything out of its *own* germ, and not from any other quarter.

(6.) He produces all things together which ought to be together.

(7.) He produces all things by their own steps of gradation, so that one thing makes way for another.

(8.) Finally, he does not produce useless things.

In imitation of the Sun and its operation :—

(1.) Let there be only one teacher for a school, or at least for a class.

(2.) In one subject, let there be but one author.

(3.) Let one and the same labour be expended on the whole of the pupils present.

(4.) Let all disciplines and tongues be taught according to one and the same method.

(5.) Let all things be taught from the foundation, briefly and nervously.

(6.) Let all things be joined together in teaching which are in themselves connected.

(7.) Let all things advance by indissoluble steps, so that everything taught to-day may give firmness and stability to what was taught yesterday, and point the way to the work of the morrow.

(8.) Let everything that is useless be eliminated from the teaching.

There is a curious parallelism here attempted between the operations of the sun and of the schoolmaster, but always fanciful, and frequently strained. I have no doubt that the analogies of Nature frequently suggested methods to the mind of Comenius, and on the other hand, that good school-methods suggested to him the modes of operations of Nature as they presented themselves to the non-scientific apprehension of the time.

Comenius now proceeds to apply the above eight principles or rules to school-management, and throws what he has to say into the form of problems to be solved.

First Problem.—*How can one teacher suffice for any number of pupils whatsoever?*

A large number of pupils is in itself an advantage to both teacher and taught, stimulating the former and exciting sympathy in work and emulation in studies. To facilitate the teaching of a large class by one instructor, certain rules, however, must be attended to.

(1.) The whole class should be divided into certain tribes or decuriæ, and over each of these an inspector or decurio should be appointed. (2.) The teacher should teach all at once, and none separately, either in the school or privately—all together and at once (*simul et semel*). For this it is necessary that he possess the art of fixing the attention of all on himself, and of never saying anything except to listeners, and never teaching anything save when all are attending. The decuriones will be a great aid in securing the attention of their various divisions, but the master himself should—

Endeavour always to present some teaching which will please and profit the pupils.

At the beginning of every fresh task, he should prepare the minds of his pupils, by commending to them the new matter, either by showing its coherence with what has already been put before, or by starting such questions regarding it as will show their ignorance, and make them more eager to know.

He should take up such a position, somewhat raised, as will enable him to control the eyes and fix the attention of all on himself.

He should always assist attention by representing what he teaches to the *eyes* of the class.

He should every now and then interrupt his teaching by sudden questions as to what he has just said, or as to the steps by which he has reached what he is telling them.

If he fails to get an answer from the boy of whom he has asked a question, he should leap to the second, third, tenth, thirtieth, for an answer, *without repeating the question.*

Sometimes, if one or two fail, he should ask the whole class, praising the boy who first answers.

When the lesson is finished an opportunity should be given to the pupils to ask public questions of the master, either regarding the lesson then given, or any previous one.

By following these expedients in teaching, the habit of attention is formed in the pupils, not only for the passing occasion, but for their whole lives.

The objection may be made that this class-teaching is not sufficient: that there must be examination of the individual exercises written, and of the lessons committed to memory; and that for this many pupils demand much time. To this Comenius replies that it is not necessary that all be always heard, nor that all the exercise-books be always examined. The decurions will examine each the work of his own division. The master himself, as supreme inspector, will pick out an exercise to examine here and there, especially directing himself to those whom he distrusts. As to memory-tasks, one, or two, or three should be called upon, all the rest listening, to repeat what has been prescribed. Each need say a portion only. In this way, by the examination of a few in no set order, the master will cause all to prepare their work. So in dictation, call on one or two to read out what they have written in a distinct voice, while the rest look on their own books and correct their own exercises, the master pouncing down on one here and there to see that the corrections are being honestly made.

In the correction of written exercises more labour seems to be demanded; but here too, following the same line, a plan is found of abbreviating work. In translation exercises, for example, one boy should rise up and challenge an antagonist. When he has risen, the challenger should read his translation, clause by clause, all the rest attentively listening, the teacher, or if not, a decurion, standing by to inspect the spelling. When he has read a sentence, let him pause, and let the antagonist then point out any error he may have noted. Then let the other members of that decuria make their criticisms, and thereafter the whole class, and finally the teacher himself. Meanwhile let all the pupils look at their translations and make corrections, with the exception of the antagonist, who preserves his own exercise unaltered, to be in its turn subjected to criticism. That sentence being thoroughly corrected, go to the next, and so to the end. Then let the antagonist read off his own exercise in like manner, under the inspection of his challenger, who will see that he has made no corrections. Then call out another couple, and so on according to the time available, the decurions taking care that those in their own decuriæ correct their exercises. In this way it will happen that the labour of the master will be saved; that all will be instructed, and none neglected; the attention of all will be sharpened; all will share in whatever is said to one; the variety of phrases *inapplicable* will form and strengthen the judgment as to the matter of the exercise, and promote facility in the language. A few pairs having·had their errors corrected, it will be seen that there are now no more errors remaining. The rest of the time may be given to the class as a whole, for the answering of questions put by the pupils, and for allowing any one to bring forward any turn of expression which he may think better than that adopted.

The above remarks are made with special reference to the version, but they are equally applicable to exercises in Rhetoric, Logic, etc.

Thus Comenius solves the problem how one teacher can suffice for one hundred pupils.

SECOND PROBLEM.—The second rule of procedure yields this question, *How can all be taught from the same books?* By requiring the pupils to have the same editions, the same lexicons, grammar, etc. It is desirable to publish school-books which will contain, simply and popularly put, all that it is necessary to teach in school. Comenius advocates the dialogue form for school-books, because they excite the interest and retain the attention better than the didactic form, supporting his preference by the fact that our lives are spent in conversation, and dialogues are easily repeated. He would further paint on the school-room walls the skeleton or outline of the contents of the books in use.

THIRD PROBLEM.—The third rule of procedure yields this question : *How is it possible that all the scholars may be made to do the same thing at the same time?* By beginning school-work only once a year, and arranging it in such a way that every month, week, day, and even hour, shall have its own proper task.

FOURTH PROBLEM.—The fourth rule yields the following question : *How can all things be taught according to one and the same method?* There is only one natural method for all studies—sciences, arts, and languages,—and this will be shown in the sequel, and has already been laid down in its principles.

FIFTH PROBLEM.—The fifth rule yields the question : *How can the understanding of many things be set forth in few words?* Fundamental things are to be taught, and this not by means of large books or much talk, but by means of well-selected words and principles, and rules easy to be understood, and fruitful in their character. A gold coin is of more value than a hundred leaden ones. As Seneca says, 'Precepts are to be sown in the mind as seed is sown in the soil, and it is not necessary that they be numerous, but efficacious.'

SIXTH PROBLEM.—The sixth rule yields the question : *How can instruction be given so as to do two or three things at the same time?* A tree grows in every part at once ; so with an animal. In school we must imitate Nature, guided by the following general canon :—'Always and everywhere let the related be taught in conjunction with its correlate'—*e.g.* words with things, reading with writing, etc.

Above all, never teach words without things, even in the vernacular, and whatever the pupils see, hear, taste, or touch, let them name. The tongue and the intelligence should advance on parallel lines. And from this it follows that a boy should never read or recite anything which he does not understand; and it further follows that all authors are to be banished from school except those who give a knowledge of useful things.

So with reading and writing : let boys be taught not merely to read, but to express themselves in writing at the same time—an exercise which is pleasing to them, and very valuable. But the exercises should not be exercises of style merely, but should have reference to the department of knowledge they are studying—*e.g.* histories of the inventors of arts, and the places and times in which arts flourished, or, it may be, exercises of imitation.

Comenius holds also that boys should teach as well as learn, and that sportive imitations of the serious work of life might advantageously be introduced into the school, side by side with serious employments—*e.g.* the boys should be encouraged to form themselves into a semblance of political and social order, with the titles of King, Councillors, Chancellor, Marshal, Secretaries, Ambassadors, and so forth.

SEVENTH PROBLEM.—The seventh rule yields the question : *How can all things be prosecuted step by step?* Comenius here refers the reader to those parts of the methodology which deal specially with gradual step-by-step progress.

EIGHTH PROBLEM.—The eighth rule yields the question : *How shall we avoid and remove causes of retardation in our progress ?*

The answer to this is, ' By a wise neglect.' It is not the quantity of things known, but the real utility of them, that is of importance. Therefore, the school should neglect whatever is unnecessary, whatever is alien to the pupil or subject of study, and whatever is too detailed. Unnecessary knowledge is all that knowledge which is unnecessary to virtue and religion, and all without which learning is attainable—*e.g.* the names of heathen idols and accounts of pagan rites, and all comic and other writings which are immoral in their character. Alien things are such as are foreign to the natural tendency of the scholar. One boy has a turn for theoretic and another for practical study, one for music, another for grammar and logic, and so on. It is a waste of time to employ a boy in music who is naturally incapacitated for that subject, while he has strong aptitude for another.

Too much detail is also condemned. It is absurd, for example, to occupy classes, which are studying natural history or botany, with all the differences of plants and animals ; or when arts are the subjects of study, with the names of all the tools. The school has to do with the generic, at most with the leading differences ; if these are fully and solidly given, the rest will be acquired through the occasions of life. Among things too detailed are such school-books as *full* lexicons, which only serve to confuse and overload a boy.

Comenius having dealt thus generally with the Art of School Teaching, next proceeds to apply Method in detail to the teaching of the three branches of all sound education, viz., Knowledge, *i.e.* Sciences and Arts, including Language (*Eruditio*), Morality (*Virtus*), and Piety (*Religio*).

I. METHOD AS APPLIED TO KNOWLEDGE.

(*a.*) THE SCIENCES.

Science is the knowledge of things—the things of external sight and of internal sight. As for the former are needed the eye, the object, and light, which are the conditions of vision, so for the latter are needed the eye of the mind, an object, viz. all things, and the light of attention. It is essential to a knowledge of the sciences, viz. :—

1. *That the eye of the mind be pure.*

This is a gift of God, speaking generally; but we have it in our own power not to suffer the looking-glass of our mind to be dulled with dust, and its brightness obscured. The dust referred to is idle, useless, and vain mental occupations. Unless Reason also preside over observation, we shall pick up dust and chaff instead of grain.

2. *It is necessary that objects be presented to the eye of the mind.*

Everything should be presented to as many senses
as possible, namely, visible things to sight, audible
things to hearing, odorous things to the smelling sense,
sapid things to the taste, tangible to the touch, and
when things have reference to more senses than one,
they should be presented to all those senses.   For the
beginning of knowledge is from pure sense, not from
words; and truth and certitude are testified to by the
evidence of the senses.   The senses are the most faithful
stewards of the memory.   Horace truly says (*De Art.
Poet.* l. 180) :—

> ' Segnius irritant animos demissa per aurem,
>   Quam quae sunt oculis subjecta fidelibus, et quae
>   Ipse sibi tradit spectator.'

Failing the objects themselves, diagrams and pictures
should be resorted to.

3. *There must also be the light of attention.*

Without this objects would be in vain presented; by
means of it the learner receives all things with an
intelligence alive, and as it were gaping, to receive
instruction.

4. *There must be a method of so presenting things that
a firm impression shall be made.*

Objects must be placed before the eyes, not far off,
but at a fit distance, directly in front, and not obliquely,
in such a way that the whole object will be seen all
round, then part by part, and from the beginning to
the end, in order.   Each individual character should
be fixed upon till everything has been seized correctly
by its differences.

These considerations as to the teaching of the sciences yield nine very useful rules :—

1. *Whatever is to be known must be taught.* Perfunctory or negligent treatment of subjects will not suffice.

2. *Whatever is taught should be taught as a thing present to the pupil, and of a certain and definite use.*

The things around us and their relations to life are to be taught.

3. *Whatever is taught should be taught directly, and not in a roundabout way—i.e.* the thing itself, and not elaborate and confused language about a thing.

4. *Everything should be so taught as to show* HOW *it is and becomes—i.e. per causas.*

To know a thing in its causes is true science.

5. *Priora should come first, and posteriora next; and, therefore, whatever is presented as an object of knowledge should be presented first generally, and thereafter in its parts.*

6. *All the parts of a thing should be known, even the more minute, none being omitted : also, its order, situation, and connection with other things.*

7. *All things should be taught successively, but only one at a time.*

8. *Each point should be insisted on until it is comprehended.*

9. *The differences of things should be carefully taught, so that there may be a distinct knowledge. Qui bene distinguit, bene docet.* The variety and the truth of things depends on their differences.

It is true that all preceptors are not equally expert

in applying method, and to assist them, therefore, the sciences to be taught should be expounded in text-books, according to the true method of teaching.

(*b.*) THE ARTS (*exclusive of Foreign Languages*).

By the Arts Comenius means Reading the vernacular, Writing, Singing, Composition and Rhetoric, Logic or Reasoning. His remarks are, however, applicable to teaching in Technical Schools in the strict and proper sense of the term technical. [By 'Technical' instruction is, in these days, very generally meant instruction merely in the elements of physical science generally; at other times, in the elements of science in specific reference to certain arts or trades; at other times, but this rarely, training to specific arts in workshop-schools.]

How are youth to be trained to the *praxis* of things?

The answer to this is given in eleven canons :—

1. *Let things that have to be done be learned by doing them.*

Mechanics and artists do not teach their apprentices by disquisitions, but by giving them something to do. They are taught to make anything by making it, to paint by painting. to dance by dancing, etc. So we should teach to write by writing, to read by reading, to sing by singing, to reason by reasoning, etc.

2. *Let there always be present to the pupil a definite form and norm of the things to be done.*

The pupil can, as yet, do nothing of himself, and must have something to imitate. To ask a boy to make straight lines, squares, circles, drawings, etc., without setting examples before him, and without giving him the requisite tools, is cruelty.

3. *Let the use of instruments be pointed out in reality rather than in words; that is to say, by example rather than by precept.*

Our grammars consist of precepts and rules, and exceptions to rules, and limitations of exceptions, so that boys are overwhelmed and stupefied. Mechanics do not proceed in this way with their apprentices, but let them look at the products of the workshop, and put tools in their hands, and train them to imitate their masters, admonishing them more by example than by words if they see them go wrong. So it is also that children learn to walk, speak, run, and play, viz., by imitation. Precepts require application and vigour of mind, whereas the feeblest are assisted by examples. As Quintilian says, ' *Longum et difficile iter est per praecepta, breve et efficax per exempla.*'

4. *Let practice begin from the elements, and not from completed works.*

A carpenter does not start his pupil with the building of turrets or citadels, but requires him to hold an axe, cut wood, bore holes, drive nails, etc. So acts a painter with his pupil. Nor do we teach to read by placing a book before a child, but by giving him first the letters, then syllables, then words. In grammar, accordingly, we should give the tyro first single words, then two together to be declined, then simple sentences, then sentences with two and three clauses, till we bring him to the full period and the complete oration. In rhetoric, we should exercise in synonyms, in attaching appropriate epithets, in varying sentences by periphrasis, and so gradually bring the pupil to the more ornamental parts of style.

5. *Let the first exercises of tyros be in a known subject.*

This has been, in a former part of this treatise, laid down. Pupils should not be burdened with things remote from their age, powers of comprehension, and present condition: this is to cause them to struggle with shadows. That the boy may understand things, take examples, not from Cicero, or Virgil, or theologians, etc., but from things familiar,—his book, clothes, trees, house, school, etc. We in this way connect what has to be learned with what is already known, and make remembrance and the further extension of knowledge in the same direction easy. In rules, the application of a rule being shown from a first, second, or third *known* example, the boy will find it easy to imitate it in all others.

6. *Let imitation be always for a time the direct and close imitation of a prescribed rule; at a later stage the imitation may be freer.*

7. *Let the things which are given as patterns be as perfect as possible, so that we may be able to pronounce him perfect in his art who adequately imitates them.*

This applies, not merely to the perfection of lines, drawings, etc., to be imitated, but also to instruction in rules, which should be very brief, very lucid and intelligible.

8. *Let the strictest accuracy in imitation be insisted on in the first attempts, so that there may not be the slightest departure from the norm.*

This is necessary, because the beginnings are the foundations of all that follows, and any looseness in the foundations will tell throughout. There should be no haste; he gets on fast enough who does not wander from the road.

9. *Let any deviation from accuracy be corrected by the master there and then; but let him add observations by way of rules or directions.*

Arts are to be taught by examples rather than by rules; but very brief and lucid rules, exhibiting what is implicit in the examples, should be given—*e.g.* from what point to start the task, at what point to aim, in what way to advance.

10. *A perfect discipline in an art consists in synthesis and analysis.*

That is to say, a pupil must first, beginning with the most simple forms, be taught to construct in accordance with a perfect pattern. This synthetic exercise, with the help of such rules as have been formerly adverted to as requisite, having been sufficiently practised, the pupils should be introduced to the analysis of the work of others, that they may see the art in full operation, and discuss the principles which underlie successful work.

11. *Exercises should be continued till the habit of the art has been formed.*

(*c.*) LANGUAGES.

Languages are taught, not as themselves a part of learning or wisdom, but as the instrument of acquiring learning and wisdom, and communicating them to others. All tongues are not to be learned. This would be as impossible as it would be useless, and interfere with the time due to acquiring a knowledge of things. Necessary languages, accordingly, are alone to be learned,—*first*, the vernacular; *secondly*, the languages of neighbouring nations; *thirdly*, Latin, as the common tongue of the learned. Theologians will study Greek and Hebrew, and physicians Greek and Arabic.

Nor should the whole of any language be learned, but only what is necessary. It is not necessary to learn to speak Greek and Hebrew as if we had to converse in them, but only to learn them so far as is needful for the understanding of what is written in these tongues. The study of languages should run parallel with the study of things, especially in youth, for we desire to form men, not parrots.

From which it follows that words that denote things are not to be learned separately and individually, because things do not exist separately, but are seen as being here or there, as doing this or that, as conjoined with other things. This is the key to the *Janua Linguarum.*[1] In this book, only necessary words are employed, contrary to the practice of some amplifiers of the book, who stuff it with unusual words, and words,

---

[1] See the chapter under this heading in the sequel.

too, away from the ordinary apprehension of the young. And those make a similar mistake who occupy the minds of the young with great authors such as Cicero, instead of with language that treats of boyish things, reserving adult things for the adult. Knowledge of language advances, like the intellect, step by step; Nature does not proceed *per saltum,* nor does art when it imitates Nature. A boy must be taught to walk before he can be taught to dance. He must prattle before he speaks, and he must speak before he can make an oration. The following eight rules will make the acquisition of languages short and easy :—

1. *Let every language be learnt separately.*

First, the vernacular is to be learned, and then a neighbouring modern tongue, then Latin, and thereafter Greek, Hebrew, etc. : and, to prevent confusion, let them be learned always one after the other, and *not together.* When a firm hold has been got of each, they may, with great benefit, be compared.

2. *Let every language have a definite space of time assigned to it.*

As we must have respect to things, and as the vernacular is more closely and naturally allied with *things* which present themselves gradually to the intellect, it demands more time than any other tongue,—probably eight or ten years; that is to say, the whole of infancy, and part of boyhood. Then should follow a modern tongue, which can be sufficiently acquired in one year; then Latin, which may be despatched in two years; Greek in one, and Hebrew in half a year.

3. *Let every language be learned by practice rather than by precept.*

That is to say, by reading, re-reading, transcribing, attempting imitations by hand and tongue—all as often as possible.

4. *Let precepts, however, aid and strengthen practice.*

This has been adverted to in the last chapter, and is specially necessary in the acquisition of the learned tongues, though applicable also to spoken languages.

5. *Let the precepts of language be grammatical, not philosophical.*

That is to say, let them state the what and the how of a usage, and not enter with subtlety into the why of phrases and forms of syntax.   This kind of speculation is philosophical, not philological.

6. *Let the precepts of a new language be first known as differences from languages already known.*

It is not only useless to teach what is common to a new language with one already acquired, but it is confusing and overwhelming.   In Greek grammar there is a very great deal which is common to it with Latin, and only those things are to be taught in which Greek differs from Latin, the rest being assumed.   A very few leaves will suffice to hold all that is new Greek syntax, and everything will be thus more distinct to the pupil, easier, and more firmly got hold of.

7. *Let the first exercises in a new tongue be about subjects already known to the pupil.*

Not with a view to things, but with a view to the more rapid command of words.   The Catechism or

Bible History, for example, where the matter is known and the same words frequently recur, would be good books for the purpose; or the *Vestibulum* and *Janua*.

8. *Let all tongues be learned by one and the same method.*

Comenius next sets forth the different steps in learning a language, and divides the time into four ages :—

The prattling age of Infancy, with its corresponding book—the *Vestibulum*.

The Boy age—the age of speaking correctly, with its corresponding book—the *Janua*.

The Juvenile age—when elegant speech may be acquired, with its corresponding book—the *Atrium* [here called the *Palatium*].

The Virile age—the age of nervous speech, with its corresponding book, being extracts from good authors —the *Thesaurus* [afterwards called the *Palatium*].

The *Vestibulum* should consist of little sentences, in which several hundreds of the more common words should be conveyed, with an appendix of the declensions and conjugations. The *Janua* should contain all the usual words in a language; about 8000 should be given in short sentences naturally expressed, with an appendix of short and clear grammar rules. The *Palatium* should contain treatises on all sorts of things, in every kind of phraseology, with attention to elegance of diction, accompanied with marginal notes on authors from whom passages have been taken, and rules for varying words and phrases in a thousand ways. The

Thesaurus will be composed of the classical authors themselves, with rules for observing and collecting nervous phraseology and varying idioms.   A list of authors not read, but who may be afterwards useful, should be added.

 Comenius would not put a dictionary of a language into the hands of a beginner, but would have certain subsidiary books constructed for each stage in Latin—a Latin-vernacular and vernacular-Latin vocabulary for those using the *Vestibulum ;* an etymological lexicon for those using the *Janua ;* a lexicon of phrases, synonyms, etc. (Latino-Latin, Græco-Greek), for those using the *Palatium ;* and finally, a *Promptuarium Catholicon* (vernacular and Latin) for those using the *Thesaurus,* and in which everything may be found which will exhibit the resources of the language.

II. METHOD APPLIED TO MORALITY.

As yet Method has been thought of in relation only to knowledge—to science, arts, including language—to which we may apply the remark of Seneca, ' *Non discere ista debemus sed didicisse.'*   They are in truth only preparatory to the true end, the pursuit of philosophy, whereby we may become elevated, strong, high-minded. We, as Christians, designate this end of education, morality and piety, or virtue and religion, instruction in which has to be introduced into all schools.   Sixteen rules for the instilling of morality may be given :—

1. *All the virtues, without exception, are to be implanted in youth.*

This is essential to a harmony of the moral nature —*harmonia morum.*

2. *But, first of all, the primary or cardinal virtues have to be implanted, viz., Prudence, Temperance, Fortitude, and Justice.*

Firm foundations must be laid for a building, that all the various parts may cohere well with the basis.

3. *By learning the true differences of things, and their values, pupils will be instructed in* PRUDENCE.

Sound judgment is the foundation of all virtue. We must know the precise nature of each thing if we are to discern the good from the bad, the desirable from the undesirable.

4. *During the whole period of instruction let the young be taught* TEMPERANCE *in eating and drinking, sleep and waking, labour and play, speaking and keeping silence.*

The golden rule is *Ne quid nimis.*

5. *Let boys learn* FORTITUDE *by overcoming themselves; to wit, by checking their desire to run about and play beyond the proper time, or at the wrong time; by restraining their impatience, their grumbling, their anger.*

Man is a rational animal, and he must be guided by reason if he is to be truly king over his own actions. But inasmuch as all boys are not fully capable of reasoning, they will be taught self-command by being accustomed to do the will of another rather than their own, by promptly obeying, in all things, those above them.

Under Fortitude we include an honourable frankness of speech and tolerance of labour.

Ingenuous frankness is acquired by frequent conversation with honourable men, and by doing in their sight what has been ordered. Aristotle so educated Alexander that in his twelfth year he conversed with all sorts of men intelligently, kings and ambassadors, learned and unlearned, townspeople and rustics, and could contribute something apposite to the conversation, either in the way of question or answer. Conversation with their elders, becomingly and modestly conducted, should be encouraged in the young, and their faults of manner thus corrected.

The young will acquire tolerance of labour if they are always doing something or other—either work or play. Perpetual but moderate occupation of mind and body give rise to industrious and active habits. ' *Generosos animos labor nutrit,*' says Seneca.

6. JUSTICE *will be learned by doing harm to no one, by giving to each his own, by avoiding lying and deceit, by being generally serviceable and amiable.*

Under Justice is included promptitude and alacrity in serving others.

The inherent vice of selfishness is thereby counteracted, and regard for the public good engendered. The boy has to be taught the scope of our life,—that we are born not for ourselves alone, but for God and our fellow-men.

7. *The formation of the virtues should begin from tender years, before vices take possession of the soul.*

If good seed be not sown, the field will still produce, but the produce will, in that case, be weeds and tares. Begin from the earliest years to plough and sow, if you would reap a harvest.

8. *The virtues are learned by constantly doing honourable things.*

Things to be known are learned by knowing, things to be done by doing; therefore, obedience is to be learned by obeying, abstinence by abstaining, truthfulness by speaking the truth, constancy by being constant, and so forth.

9. *Let the examples of a well-constituted life always shine as a lamp before children—the examples of parents, nurses, teachers, school-fellows.*

Boys are as imitative as apes, and learn to imitate long before they learn to know. Historical examples are good, but living examples are better.

10. *Nevertheless, precepts and rules of life are to be added to examples.*

The precepts of Scripture and the sayings of wise men should be taught.

11. *Children are to be most diligently guarded against intercourse with bad companions, lest they be infected.*

Vicious example is a poison to the mind, whether it enter by the eye or ear. In consequence of our depraved nature, evil things cling with wonderful facility and tenacity. Idleness leads to evil, and hence the importance of constant occupation, be it work or play.

12. *Discipline is necessary for the purpose of withstanding immoral habits.*

By discipline is meant reproof by words and chastisement by stripes. Punishment by stripes should be reserved for moral offences. This subject is further treated of below.

III. Method as applied to Piety.

Though piety is the gift of God through the Holy Spirit, yet as the Spirit commonly acts through ordinary means—parents, teachers, and ministers of the Church, —it is right to consider the method of the duties of these instruments.

Comenius gives great prominence to this part of his Didactic, and treats of it at considerable length; but it cannot be said that *Method* in any strict application of that term is successfully exhibited in its relation to religious instruction. The chapter on this subject is in reality a series of propositions in which the order of Christian doctrinal teaching is laid down, and to some extent the manner of it. The following paragraphs contain the substance of his instructions :—

After laying down three sources of piety, viz., the Holy Scriptures, the world or nature, and ourselves (*i.e.* the natural instincts and intuitions which give a knowledge of God, and our dependence on Him), he says that there are three ways of cherishing piety, viz., meditation on the words, works, and goodness of God; prayer, which he defines to be *perpetua ad Deum suspiratio ;* and self-examination. ' Examine yourselves

whether ye be in the faith : prove your own selves'
(2 Cor. xiii. 5).

In educating children in religion we should attend
to the following rules :—

Begin in infancy : we must sow good seed.

From the very first accustom the child to express
devotion *bodily* with his eyes, hands, feet, and tongue ;
by gazing towards heaven, spreading out his palms,
bending his knees, and invoking God and Christ,
reverencing and adoring the invisible Majesty.

Let them be taught that we are here not for this life
alone, but that eternity is our goal; that our chief
aim is to be so prepared as worthily to enter eternal
habitations ; and that all we do must have the future
life in view, and that we must constantly bear in mind
the twofold destiny that awaits man hereafter.

Let them be taught that thrice happy are they who
so regulate their lives as to be worthy of dwelling with
God ; that whosoever walk with God here, will dwell
with Him everlastingly, and that by walking with God is
meant having Him constantly before our eyes, fearing
Him, and keeping His commandments.

Let them be taught to refer all things—whatsoever
they hear or see, do or suffer,—to God, mediately or
immediately.

Let them learn to occupy themselves from the
earliest years with those things that lead to God—the
reading of the Holy Scriptures, the exercises of divine
worship, and good works.

Let the Holy Scriptures be the Alpha and Omega of Christian schools.

Let whatever is learned from Scripture be referred to the three graces of Faith, Hope, and Charity; and let these graces be taught with reference to practice. These will be taught in relation to practice if the young be taught to *believe* all that God has revealed, to *do* what He commands, and to *hope* for what He promises.

Let boys be accustomed to the doing of those works commanded by Heaven, that by those works they may show forth their faith—the works, namely, of temperance, justice, compassion, patience, etc.

Let them be taught to see clearly the purposes of the benefits God confers, and of the chastisements He inflicts.

Let them be exhorted to keep the way of the Cross as the most secure way, and let care be taken that no vicious examples obstruct them in their path.

Finally, let them be taught that, since, because of the imperfection of their nature, they can do no good thing, they must rely on the perfection of Christ, the Lamb of God that taketh away the sins of the world.

The mode of dexterously doing all this in the different classes of the school has to be carefully considered.

Comenius maintains at considerable length, and with occasional eloquence, the necessity of either banishing Pagan authors from schools, or at least of using them with caution. Realists like Comenius discouraged purely classical studies, not merely because they usurped the place which ought to be assigned to the study of subjects having a practical bearing on this life, but also because they obstructed or at least did not promote, the true ends of a Christian school.

All now accept the opinion that the classical authors are to be read by boys with due caution ; but I imagine that none will be found to take the restricted view that they should be excluded altogether from schools even on religious grounds. Strict logical reasonings from a fundamental principle are justly suspected when they land us in such conclusions, and the majority of teachers are content to sacrifice logic rather than part with their common sense.

IV. On School Discipline.

The Bohemians say that 'a school without discipline is a mill without water.' For take the water away and the mill stops; take discipline away and the school lags. It does not follow from this that a school is to be a place of cries, blows, and weals ; but there must be vigilance and attention, both in the teacher and taught.

What is discipline save a certain way whereby scholars (*discipuli*) are made to be *truly* scholars ?

Let us consider, then, discipline in its end, its matter, and its form—its *cur, quando, quomodo.*

1. *The end of discipline.*—This is not the punishment of a transgressor for a fault he has committed (the done

cannot be undone), but the prevention of the recurrence
of the fault.   Accordingly, the master must execute
punishment without passion, anger, or hatred, but in
such a way that the boy under discipline will recognise
that it is done for his good, and on that account will
accept it as he would accept a disagreeable draught
from a physician.

2. *The matter of discipline.*—A severe discipline is
not to be exercised in the matter of studies, but only in
that of morals. If subjects of study are rightly arranged
and taught, they themselves attract and allure all save
very exceptional natures ; and if they are not rightly
taught, the fault is in the teacher, not the pupil. Moreover, if we do not know how to allure to study by skill,
we shall certainly not succeed by the application of
mere force. There is no power in stripes and blows
to excite a love of literature, but a great power, on
the contrary, of generating weariness and disgust. A
musician does not dash his instrument against a wall,
or give it blows and cuffs, because he cannot draw music
from it, but continues to apply his skill till he extracts
a melody. So by our skill we have to bring the minds
of the young into harmony, and to the love of studies,
if we are not to make the careless unwilling and the
torpid stolid. A spur and stimulus are often needed,
but a sharp word or a public reproof or the praise of
others who are doing well, will generally suffice.

Those who transgress in moral matters are to be
more seriously dealt with. Impiety, for example, such
as blasphemy and obscenity, and all that is done

against the law of God, constitute serious offences, and can be expiated only by a severe chastisement. Contumacy and deliberate perversity, wilful non-doing of what the pupil knows ought to be done—are to be punished. Also, pride, envy, and sloth.

3. *The how of discipline.*—The sun (regarded by Comenius as the cause of atmospheric changes) *always* gives forth light and warmth, often rain and wind, rarely thunder and lightning. So (1.) The teacher should always shine as an example, in his own person and conduct, of all he requires from others. (2.) By words of instruction, exhortation, and occasionally reproof, he should *labour* to sustain discipline, being most careful that all he says verily comes from a parental interest in and affection for his pupils, for if the pupils do not see this they harden their hearts against discipline. (3.) If any pupil is of so unhappy a disposition that these gentler methods fail, more violent remedies should be applied, lest anything should be left undone before utterly despairing of a boy; but great care has to be exercised that we do not resort to extreme remedies except in extreme cases. *Extrema in extremis.* The whole object of discipline, we must never forget, is to form in those committed to our charge a disposition worthy of the children of God.[1]

---

[1] Speaking of the improvement of schools, Professor Eilhardus Lubinus says:—'Prorsus sentio virgas et verbera servilia illa instrumenta ac ingeniis minimé convenientia minimé in scholis adhibenda sed procul removenda esse et admovenda mancipiis et servilis animi nequam servis.'

This is the end of Method as applied to Knowledge, Virtue, and Religion, and it seems to be a fit place to introduce some precepts of Comenius which are given in the *Dissertatio de sermonis Latini studio.*

PRACTICAL HINTS TO THE TEACHER OF A CLASS.

1. Let the teacher not teach as much as he is able to teach, but only as much as the learner is able to learn.

2. Whatever difficulty and trouble scholastic labours bring, let these be borne by the teacher, nothing being left to the pupil except the desire to imitate, and the acquisition of facility in imitating.

3. Whatever teachers wish their pupils to know, let them set forth that thing with the greatest possible perspicuity.

4. Whatever teachers wish their pupils to do, let them point out the way by themselves doing it.

5. Let nothing ever seem so easy as to relieve the teacher of the duty of striving, in various ways, to make it more perspicuous and more easy of imitation.

6. Never let the pupils be overburdened with a mass of things to be learned.

7. Three things always are to be formed in the pupil, viz., mind, hand, and tongue.

8. And these three come one after the other. It is the easiest of the three to understand anything; the next is to imitate it in writing; the most difficult, and that which is nearest perfection, is to be able to express it with the tongue. This is applicable to arts and

sciences as well as language. Let the teachers therefore give heed that, whatever they desire their pupils to learn easily and successfully, shall advance by these gradations without confusion.

9. Always let examples precede, as being the matter of instruction; let precepts and rules follow, as the form.

10. Never dismiss any subject which has been begun, until it is thoroughly finished. Let the teacher never take more matter for a lesson than can be both set forth and expounded within the same hour, and impressed on the intellect and memory of the pupils, during that same hour, by fit examples.

11. Let the first foundations of all things be thoroughly laid, unless you wish the whole superstructure to totter.

12. Accordingly, whatever the teacher begins to teach, let him give pains to see that it is accurate, and so firmly learnt that those things which follow can be safely built on the top of it.

13. If anything has been wrongly apprehended, take care that it do not drive roots into the mind, but that it be immediately torn up.

14. Whatever is taught, let it be taught accurately, that it may not cause misconception.

15. Let similar diligence be applied in giving exercises in style (composition).

16. To insure this, let the example, which is given for imitation, be unexceptionable, and let the imitation of it be attempted only in the master's presence, and under his inspection.

17. By far the greatest abridgment of labour is for the teacher not to teach one boy alone, but many together.

18. In order that this may be done, two things are necessary :—

(*a.*) That those pupils only be admitted into the same class who are of equal advancement, and that they be admitted at the same time.

(*b.*) That skill be used, with a view to secure that none of the pupils shall be ignorant of that which is taught to all.

19. To secure this, the following things must be attended to :—

(*a.*) Let the teacher take care that he always brings to his class something in the way of instruction likely to please and to profit.

(*b.*) At the beginning of every task the minds of the pupils should be prepared for the instruction, either by commending to their attention the subject to be taught ; or by putting questions on what has been already taught, which lead up to the new by showing its coherence with the old ; or by bringing out their ignorance of the subject, so that they may receive the explanation of it with greater avidity.

(*c.*) Let the master stand in a somewhat elevated position, where he can see all round him and so prevent any one from doing anything else but looking at him.

. (*d.*) Let him always assist the attention of the pupils by presenting everything, in so far as possible, to the senses (hearing, seeing, etc.).

(*e.*) Let the teacher sharpen the attention of the pupils by occasionally asking one here and there, 'What was it I just said?' 'Repeat it,' etc.

(*f.*) If any one who has been asked a question fails, let the teacher go to the second, third, tenth, thirtieth, *without repeating the question.*

(*g.*) If one or another cannot do it, let him ask the question of the whole class, and praise publicly the one who answers first and best ; and

(*h.*) When the lesson is finished, let an opportunity be given to pupils of asking the teacher questions whether with reference to the lesson then given or to any previous lesson.

These precepts in the art of teaching are not given for the sake of the school alone, but because they promote habits in the pupil which are of value in after life.

Fourth Section.

ON THE GENERAL ORGANISATION OF A SCHOOL SYSTEM.

A CERTAIN fixed time ought to be set apart for the complete education of youth, at the end of which they may go forth from school to the business of life, truly instructed, truly moral, truly religious.

The time that is required for this is the whole period of youth, that is to say, from birth to manhood, which is fully attained in twenty-four years. Dividing the twenty-four years into periods of six years each, we ought to have a school suited to each period, viz., the school of—

1. Infancy :—the mother's lap up to six years of age.

2. Boyhood :—*ludus literarius*, or vernacular public school.

3. Adolescence :—the Latin School or Gymnasium.

4. Youth :—the University (*Academia*), and travel.

The Infant School should be found in every house, the Vernacular School in every village and community, the Gymnasium in every province, and the University in every kingdom or large province.

In these various schools the same things will be

taught, each subject being adapted to the stage of progress; in the earlier stages subjects will be taught more broadly and generally, in the later more in detail.

In the Mother School the external senses chiefly will be exercised in relation to objects and the distinguishing of these. In the Vernacular School the inner senses, imagination,[1] and memory will be exercised along with their executory organs, the tongue and hand, by means of reading, writing, drawing, singing, counting, measuring, weighing, and learning by heart. In the Gymnasium the intellect and judgment will be formed by means of dialectic, grammar, rhetoric, and the 'what' and 'why' of the real sciences and arts. In the University those things will be taught which depend on the Will of man and reduce the mind to harmony, *e.g.* Theology, Mental Philosophy, Medicine (*i.e.* knowledge of the vital functions of the Body), Jurisprudence.

That this is the true method of procedure is manifest; for first external things are *impressed* on the senses, then the mind seeks to *express* what it has received by reproducing the images of things in memory, and by the tongue and hand. Intelligence thereafter applies itself to what has been so acquired, and compares and weighs that it may learn the reasons and causes of things, thereby promoting the understanding of things and judgments regarding them. Finally, the Will seeks to establish its sovereignty over all things. To interfere with this order is to trifle with the whole subject, and yet this is what those do who introduce boys to

[1] *i.e.* the representative and reproductive imagination.

Logic, Ethics, Poetry, Rhetoric, before they have an adequate knowledge of the realities of sense.

Again, the Mother School and the Vernacular School will train all the population of both sexes; the Gymnasium will train those boys who aim at being something higher than artisans; and the University will form the future teachers and guides of others, so that there may never be wanting for the Church, School, or State, fit governors. These grades of schools find their analogy in the spring, summer, autumn, and winter of the year. But all these things have to be fully developed; and this Comenius now proceeds to do.

I. THE IDEA OF THE MOTHER SCHOOL.

In the Infant School (which is the family) the elements have to be taught of everything necessary to the building-up of the life of man, and we shall show that this is possible by running over the different departments of knowledge.

(*a.*) *Metaphysics.*—Conception in infants is general and confused; they do not distinguish things according to kind, but general terms are familiar to them and arise out of ordinary observation, viz., Something, Nothing, Is, Is-not, So, Otherwise, Where, When, Like, Unlike, etc., which things are the foundations of Metaphysics.

(*b.*) *Physics.*—In this infant stage the child will learn the rudiments of natural knowledge; he learns to know water, earth, fire, rain, snow, ice, stone, iron, tree, grass, bird, fish, ox, etc. etc., and the parts of his own body.

(*c.*) The beginnings of Optics he learns when he learns to name light, darkness, and the principal colours.

(*d.*) Astronomy he begins when he learns to name sun, moon, star, constellation, and the rising and setting of these.

(*e.*) The beginnings of Geography are learned when the child understands what a mountain is, a plain, a valley, a river, a village, a city, a state.

(*f.*) Chronology is learned in its rudiments in learning what an hour is, a day, a week, a month, a year, yesterday, to-day, and to-morrow, etc.

(*g.*) History he learns in learning what has recently happened, and the way in which it happened, and how this or that man conducted himself.

(*h.*) Arithmetic he learns by finding out the much and the little, by counting up to 10, and by the simplest forms of addition and subtraction.

(*i.*) The rudiments of Geometry are learned in discovering what is great and small, long and short, broad and narrow, thick and thin, a line, a circle, etc., and the ordinary measures.

(*j.*) Statics are learned in observing the light and heavy, and by balancing things.

(*k.*) Mechanics are learned by causing the children to carry things from one place to another, to arrange things, to build and take to pieces, to tie and untie. All such things, the young delight to do, and they have merely to be encouraged and directed in doing them.

(*l.*) The beginnings even of Dialectic are taught by question and answer, and by requiring direct and adequate answers to interrogations.

(*m.*) Grammar is acquired by the child in its elements through the right articulating of his mother-tongue, letters, syllables, words.

(*n.*) Rhetoric is acquired, in its beginnings, by hearing the use of metaphors in ordinary conversation, and of the rising and falling inflection in speech.

(*o.*) The foundation of a taste for poetry is laid by learning little verses, chiefly of a moral kind.

(*p.*) The daily exercises of household piety, including the singing of easy psalms and hymns, will give the elements of music.

(*q.*) The rudiments of Economics are furnished by noting the relations of father, mother, domestic servant, and the parts of a house and its furnishings.

(*r.*) Of Polity less can be learned, but even in this sphere some knowledge of the civil government and the names of governors and magistrates may be acquired.

(*s.*) But above all, the foundations of Morality have to be firmly laid—by training to temperance in all things, cleanliness of habits, due reverence to superiors, prompt obedience, truthfulness, justice, charity, continual occupation, patience, serviceableness to others, civility.

(*t.*) In Religion and Piety the beginnings are to be laid. The elements of the Christian religion should be committed to memory, and the child should be trained to recognise the perpetual presence of God, his dependence on Him, and to see in Him a punisher of evil and a rewarder of good. Simple prayers should be taught, and the child led to bend the knee and fold the hands in prayer.

Such is the task of the Mother-School, of which Comenius promises to treat in more detail in a separate treatise, entitled *Informatorium Scholae Maternae.*

In this separate treatise, however, little is added to what has been already laid down. He urges his points in more detail certainly, but without adding anything new. The value of the treatise consists in its hortatory character. The more important additions are under the heads of discipline, of childish occupations, and of bodily health.

As to *discipline*, he denounces as intolerable the noise, irregularity, and licence of some families, and urges as a remedy the example of elders, and verbal reproof; but above all, encouraging words, which tell powerfully with children. In the last resort only is the rod advocated.

In the matter of *occupations*, he urges the encouragement of all kinds of sports, and especially the love of constructing buildings, etc., in imitation of what they see, which is a natural instinct of children.

The *bodily health* of the child must be a prime object, as bodily vigour is the condition of all proper mental growth. It is not enough simply to pray that our children may be healthy and vigorous. God's blessing is given to labour on our part. Even during pregnancy, the mother should keep in mind her duty to her offspring. She should devote her mind to religious exercises more than usual, avoid all excesses in eating and drinking, and all mental anxieties ; and yet she should not be idle or luxurious, but occupy herself with alacrity and cheerfulness in her usual duties.   Comenius denounces in fervent language the employment of milknurses, holding that both Nature and Divine Providence have marked out the duty of suckling as at once a maternal duty and privilege.   After the child is weaned, simple diet only should be given, such as bread, milk, butter, and some kinds of vegetables.

Books containing pictures of things should be put into the hands of little children.   This will stimulate their observation, and help them to read, especially if the names of the things drawn or painted are written under the representations.

All the work of the Mother School is to be done in the family circle.

II. The Idea of the Vernacular School.

By the Vernacular School Comenius means what we now call the Primary School, and he presumes it to be attended by children from the age of six to twelve (their thirteenth year).

The scope and aim of the Vernacular School are stated in the form of an answer to those who hold that such schools are only for girls, and those boys whose destiny in life is industrial, and who maintain that for those whose duration of education is to be more prolonged and whose aim is higher, the Latin School or Gymnasium is the proper place from the first.

It is evident, he says, that this view is opposed to all the principles that have been laid down. If it be that our duty is to instruct *all* human beings in *all* those things that have to do with human affairs, they must *all* go through the same course as long as they hold together. We desire to instruct all alike in moralities, and also to promote mutual serviceableness, and we should remove everything which can foster the disposition to appraise oneself too highly, and to look down on others. Again, we cannot venture to say of boys six years old what their ultimate destination may be. Further, he objects to the superstitious attachment to Latin—the vernacular tongue, modern tongues, and the study of things being more important. Even the Latin tongue itself will be better learned by one who knows his vernacular, and who has in learning a new language simply to adapt new names to things already known. In brief, the Vernacular School ought to teach all that will be of use for the whole of life, and this to all.

Subjects of Instruction in the Vernacular or Primary School.

1. Let the pupil learn to read all things in his own tongue, whether printed or script.

2. Let him learn to write first neatly, then quickly, then with grammatical propriety, in accordance with rules popularly expounded.

3. Let him learn arithmetic as far as necessary.

4. Let him learn to measure lengths, breadths, distances.

K

5. Let him learn to sing the more common melodies, those who have an aptitude for it being also taught the elements of harmony[1] (or notation?).

6. Let him learn by heart the psalms and hymns more commonly used in churches.

7. Let him learn to repeat with accuracy the Catechism, and important passages from Holy Writ.

8. Let him understand morality in its precepts, and by means of examples suited to his age, and let him begin the practice of it.

9. Let him understand as much of economy and polity as is necessary for the understanding of what goes on around him.

10. Let him not be ignorant of the general history of the world—its creation, fall and redemption, and its government by the wisdom of God.

11. Let him be taught general geography, and the geography of his own country more fully.

12. A general knowledge of the mechanical arts should be given, that boys may better understand the affairs of ordinary life, and that opportunities be thus given to boys to find out their special aptitudes.

The beginnings of all kinds of knowledge will thus be laid, whatever be the future destiny of the pupils.

Means of attaining the above Ends.

1. The school period being extended over six years, the school should be divided into six classes, kept apart from each other as much as possible.

---

[1] Figuralis musica.

2. Each class should have its own books, which should contain *everything* necessary for its instruction in Literature, Morals, and Religion. These books should exhaust the vernacular tongue, in so far as the naming of things within the range of a boy's apprehension and all the more usual modes of speech, are concerned. There ought to be six such books, differing in their *mode of treating* subjects, not in the subjects they treat : advancing always from the more simple to the more special and detailed. They should be carefully adapted to the age of the pupils, and should combine the pleasant with the useful. As a school has been compared to a garden, so the titles of these books might well be made attractive by reference to a garden —*e.g.* the first might be called *Violarium*, the second *Rosarium*, the third *Viridarium*, the fourth *Labyrinthus*, the fifth *Balsamentum*, and the sixth *Paradisus Animae.*

3. The school-hours should not be more than four daily—two before noon and two after noon,—thus leaving time for amusement, and for domestic duties when the children are poor.

4. The morning hours should be given to those lessons that exercise the understanding and memory, the afternoon to those which engage the voice and hand.

5. In the morning hours, the teacher will read and re-read the lesson, giving simple explanations, while all listen attentively, and will then call on certain pupils, one after the other, to read, the rest attentively following. If the lesson is prolonged, the clever boys will be

able to say it off by heart, and later on the slower boys also; for the tasks will be short, and suited to the capacity of the pupils.

6. In the afternoon, nothing new should be attempted. The repetition of the morning lesson, transcription from the printed book, and competition as to who remembers most accurately, or can sing, write, or count best. The neat transcription of the printed books is a most valuable exercise, for the lesson is thereby more thoroughly impressed on the mind through the occupation of the senses with it, and practice in correct spelling and neat writing is given. The parents also learn from these books what their children are doing at school.

In conclusion, Comenius recommends that if any boys desire to learn foreign tongues they should begin them after their tenth year, and during the latter part of their attendance at the Vernacular School. For teaching purposes, translations into the foreign language they are learning of those books which are already known to them in the vernacular tongue should be used.

III. The Idea of the Latin School, or Gymnasium.

In this school there should be an encyclopædic course, including four languages.

The course being a six years' one (from twelve years of age to eighteen), there should also be six classes.

The subjects to be taught are as follows :—

Grammar, that is to say, a thorough knowledge of

the vernacular and Latin, and such a knowledge of Greek and Hebrew as may be necessary.

Dialectic, i.e. practice in defining, distinguishing, arguing, and in resolving arguments.

Rhetoric, i.e. the power of elegant composition on any given matter.

Arithmetic.

Geometry.

Music, practical and theoretical.

Astronomy.

These are the boasted seven liberal arts which make a man a master in philosophy. Comenius would have them taught in the Gymnasium, and, in addition, the following subjects :—

Physics, including Natural History and Mineralogy, and applications to the arts.

Geography.

Chronology.

History.

Ethics, i.e. a knowledge of the virtues and vices, and of their special application to life. And, lastly,

Theology, so that youths should have, not only a thorough knowledge of the doctrines of their faith, but of the scriptural basis of them.

It is not presumed that a thorough knowledge of all these subjects can be attained in the Gymnasium.; but only that a solid foundation may be laid in them all.

To the six classes a separate name is assigned, indicating the order in which studies are to be taken up, viz., the Grammar class, the Physics class, the Mathematical class, the Ethical class, the Dialectic class, and the Rhetoric class.

The Grammar class comes first, as the key to all else. Then the Physics precedes the Mathematics, because the numbers and quantities dealt with in the former are more within the sphere of sense than they are in the latter. Mathematics is general and abstract. Ethics will deal, not merely with the *what* of morality, as in the Vernacular School, but advance to the *why*. Dialectic will take up Physical and Ethical questions with a view to the *pro* and *con.*: it will also include a short course of logic, and the principles of investigation, and sources of error. Rhetoric, or the art of fit and elegant expression, comes last, when the youth has the necessary material for writing, and its range will be confined to very brief and very clear rhetorical precepts.

It has to be remarked that in every class, History, as the eye of life, should find a place, so that all that is most memorable in the past, both in deed and word, may be known. This, so far from increasing the burden on pupils, will lighten their labours. Little text-books should be written, viz., one on Biblical History; one on natural things; one on inventions and mechanical arts; one exhibiting the most illustrious examples of virtue; one on the various customs of nations; and finally, one containing all that is most significant in the history of the world, and especially of our own country.

It is to be taken for granted that Comenius, while defining the distinctive work of each class, presumes that the work done in the classes that precede it, is still continued. Without this, how would a sufficient knowledge of language, for example, be obtained? The Dialectic and Rhetoric classes would afford special opportunities for the revision of all the work done in the classes that preceded them.

Comenius postpones the question of the special method to be followed in the Gymnasium, merely remarking that, of the four school hours, the two before noon should be devoted to that subject by which the class is named, and the two afternoon hours to history and to exercises in writing and repeating.

IV. THE IDEA OF THE UNIVERSITY (*Academia*).

Every department of knowledge should be handled in the Universities. There will be need, accordingly, of Professors learned in all arts, sciences, faculties, tongues, and also of a library for common use.

As to the method to be pursued :—

1. Only the more select minds—the flower of youth—should be sent to Universities, all others being relegated to agriculture, the workshop, or trade.

2. Each should apply himself to that line of study for which he is specially fitted, so that nothing may be done *invita Minerva*. It would be well that the destination of youth should be fixed by a leaving-examination in the Gymnasiums.

3. Minds of large mould should be stimulated to universal knowledge, that there may be a certain number

of men of universal accomplishment—πολυμαθεῖς or πάνσοφοι.

4. The University should retain only those students who are industrious, honourable, and able. Those pseudo-students, who go there to spend money and waste time, should not be tolerated.

5. Authors of every kind should be studied; but as it is impossible for all to read everything that authors have written, men, learned each in his own department, should produce books which would contain, in a systematic form, the sum of Plato, Aristotle, Cicero, Galen, etc. These systematised summaries would serve as an introduction for the use of those who were going to study these great writers, and furnish all that was necessary for those who had to devote themselves specially to other studies.

6. Of academic exercises, a very important one is public disputations: the students discussing, at an afternoon meeting, what the Professor has given in a forenoon meeting, and contributing to the subject from their own reading, and suggesting questions, while the Professor acts as president.

As regards Graduation :—

University honours should be conferred only on the worthy, and it should depend on a public inquiry by commissioners, and not on private testimony, so that Doctorships and Masterships may be conferred only on those conspicuous for their diligent pursuit of learning. The qualification of the candidates should be ascertained by public oral questioning in the theory and praxis of the subjects they have studied—*e.g.* Where is this, that, or the other passage to be found? How does it agree with this or that? Do you know any author who dissents from this view? Who? What arguments does he advance, and how are they to be met? Again in *praxis:* cases are to be put—in conscience, or in medicine, or in legal causes; the how and the why is to be put, and a variety of cases brought forward, so that it may be seen that the candidate has a thorough knowledge of his subject, and can judge wisely.

Travel with a view to education should be allowed only, as Plato says, when the hotness of youth is over, and the young man has acquired sufficient prudence and tact.

So much for the University as a teaching body; but in addition to all this there ought to be a *Schola Scholarum* or *Collegium Didacticum* founded somewhere or other; and if the foundation of such a college is impossible, learned men in all parts of the world devoted to the advancement of God's glory, should combine to prosecute researches in science, and to make new discoveries bearing on the improvement of the human race. Neither one man nor one generation is sufficient for this great task; many men jointly and in successive generations must carry on the work begun. Such a universal school would be to the rest of schools what the stomach is to the body—the living workshop, supplying sap, life, strength.

CONCLUSION.

Comenius in conclusion elaborates an analogy between his method and the Art of Printing. As the Art of Printing is to the old method of producing copies of books, so is his method of education to the methods then in use. Into this parallel we need not follow him. A greater number of pupils, he maintains, will be taught with fewer teachers; a larger proportion of pupils will be truly instructed; and many who now receive no benefit from schools will receive substantial culture. As regards teachers, again, those who are not by nature adapted to the work of instruction will, by following sound method, acquire aptitude. As an organist can play from a book, symphonies which he himself could not possibly have composed, so a school-teacher may learn to teach all subjects, if he have reduced into a schematic form, as it were, all the subjects that have to be taught, and the whole method of teaching them.

I have now given the sum of the *Great Didactic.*

———

PART II.

PART II.

METHOD IN THE TEACHING OF LANGUAGE MORE FULLY CONSIDERED.[1]

THE *Didactica Magna* does not contain all that Comenius has to say. In the prefaces to his various works there are many sagacious observations both on Methods and on Education in general. These observations apply chiefly to the teaching of language. School-instruction in the fifteenth and sixteenth centuries was substantially language-instruction; and the language chiefly, though not exclusively, taught was Latin. It was unavoidable therefore that Comenius, in applying his principles and rules of Method, should have his attention largely concentrated on the teaching of Latin. Prior to Ratich, indeed, the general interest which had been excited throughout Europe in the subject of Education had for its object, so far as schools were concerned, chiefly the current methods of teaching the Latin tongue. There was a widespread and loudly expressed dissatisfaction with the results of school-teaching. Boys and masters were alike unhappy —these as teachers, those as learners; great severity

[1] From the *Methodus Linguarum novissima fundamentis didacticis solide superstructa,* 1648.

of discipline was practised, and after all was done, and all the years of youth had been spent in the study mainly of one subject, the results were contemptible. In 1614 Eilhardus Lubinus, an eminent theologian who edited the Greek Testament in three languages, speaks in these words :—'The customary method of instruction prevalent in schools is, it seems to me, precisely what we might have expected had some one been specially hired and paid to excogitate some way whereby teachers might not introduce their pupils to a knowledge of Latin, and pupils might not be introduced, except with immense toil, unspeakable tedium, infinite loss, and the expenditure of a long period of time.

> 'Quae quoties repeto vel iniqua mente revolvo
> Concutior toties, penitusque horresco medullis.'

And again he remarks, 'When considering this matter I have, to speak the truth, been often led to think that some wicked and malign spirit—an enemy of the human race—had through the agency of some ill-omened monks originally introduced the method of instruction.' And with what result?—'The production of Germanisms, Barbarisms, Solecisms, mere abortions of Latin, dishonourings and defilements of the tongue.'

The most important, and indeed the only important, treatise by Comenius on Method, in addition to the *Didactica Magna* and the short treatise on the Mother School (the substance of which I have incorporated into the preceding analysis of the Didactica) is entitled '*Novissima Linguarum Methodus*, firmly erected on

Didactic foundations, demonstrated in special relation to the Latin Tongue, adapted with precision to the use of Schools, but also capable of application with advantage to other kinds of Studies.' This treatise was published in 1648. It consists of thirty chapters—the first five of which are occupied with the consideration of language itself, beginning, as is customary with the author, *ab ovo*, and approaching the question he has to solve in the most systematic manner. There is nothing in these chapters worth reproducing for our time. Indeed, it may almost be said that, like much of Comenius's writing, they are characterised by a wearisome, elaborate, and painfully systematic statement of commonplace. There is no penetrating light cast into any dark places.

The subsequent chapters are more instructive. The principles laid down in the *Didactica* now reappear in more special and detailed application to Latin. They are, however, reached analytically, and no longer syncretically.

Latin, Comenius maintains, is the one language to be preferred to all others for schools, because it is the vehicle not only of Roman, but of all, learning; because it is the common language of the learned; because it is an excellent introduction to the study of all tongues; and because, owing to the definiteness of its forms and syntax, it presents fewer difficulties than Greek. There is no special difficulty in learning Latin; what we want is a good method. Lubinus remarks that cooks and scullions learn in a short time more of two or three modern tongues by mixing with the people who speak them than boys at school, after the greatest effort, learn of the one language Latin.

In proceeding to consider the method hitherto followed, Comenius indirectly answers Lubinus, for he points out that a language learned *only* conversationally is imperfectly learned. When we have studied a language methodically in its forms and syntax, we then know that we know it; any other mode of study yields us only more or less of the fragments of a language, and can at best give only a superficial knowledge.

The evils which need a remedy are these :—

1. The Latin language is taught abstractly, without a prior knowledge of the things which the words denote.

It will be said that the boys already know in the vernacular the things which the Latin words denote. But it is a false conclusion that because boys know how to utter vernacular words they therefore understand them. How can it advantage a boy to get at vocabularies in which he finds such things as *Necessitas*, necessity; *Pignus*, a pledge; if he do not know what either 'necessity' or 'a pledge' means? Words should be learned in their connection with things known.

2. The second evil is driving boys into the manifold intricacies of grammar from the very first.

It is the custom of schools to treat grammar from the formal instead of from the material side. This is to count money in purse without the money. It would be less absurd if a knowledge of the grammar of the vernacular had preceded the study of Latin, in which case a knowledge of the meaning of grammatical terms and rules in relation to the matter of language would already exist in the boy's mind; but it has not yet, says Comenius, even been proposed to teach grammar in vernacular schools, and boys are plunged into the formal statements of grammar on their first beginning Latin, so that they must imagine that grammar belongs to Latin alone. To make matters worse, the Latin Grammar is written in Latin. How should we adults like, if we began to learn Arabic, to have a Grammar written in Arabic put into our hands? And yet what we with our matured powers would resent, we demand of the tender minds of boys. Not to speak of the multitude and obscurity of the rules themselves, we ask boys to struggle first with the words of a rule, then with its sense, and finally with the genius of a tongue alien to their vernacular.

3. The third evil is the practice of compelling boys to take impossible leaps, instead of carrying them forward step by step.

We introduce them from the grammar into Virgil and Cicero,—Virgil's Eclogues simply because they are short, and Cicero's select epistles—select being here also equivalent to short. The sublimity of poetic style is beyond the conception of boys, and the subject-matter of Cicero's epistles is for grown men. It will be said that this is done that boys may acquire the words,

phrases, etc., of these authors, in the expectation that
when they are older they will see their force. But why
ever separate words and things? Unhappy divorce!
Why begin to build a tower at the top? It will also be
said that the object is to put a perfect model before boys
to which they may attain. Quite right to aim at a perfect
model when the aim is practicable, and if we proceed
gradually to the highest. But a boy must go step by
step, and advancing years will bring both the occasions
and the power of learning. If Cicero himself were to
enter our schools, and find boys engaged with his
works, it seems to me that he would be either amused
or indignant. Larger things are with great advantage
postponed to lesser things, and the lesser things, if
accommodated to the age of the learners, yield greater
fruits than larger things. The eminent grammarian
Vossius speaks (Lib. vii. Gram. i.) strongly against the
folly of loading boys with a mass of rules and exceptions, affirming that it is not merely useless, but hurtful
and obstructive. The language of Scioppius, the
annotator of the *Sanctii Minerva*, is stronger and more
fervid in denunciation than that of any other writer.
And when we bear in mind the construction of the Latin
Grammars then in use,—that of Alvarus, for example,
having 500 rules and as many exceptions—we cannot
be surprised at the unanimous condemnation of the
then current methods of teaching, and the almost
universal lamentation over the wasted years of youth.

Comenius gives some account of the various proposals for reform current in his time. It was natural

that many should be driven to the conversational
method as a means of attaining a knowledge of Latin
in the intercourse of daily life. Schoolmasters were
tyrants and torturers of boys, and the instrument of
their tyranny was the Latin Grammar. Cæcilius Frey,
on the same side of the question, proposed the institution of Colleges, where all, including the servants, should
speak Latin and Greek. To these, boys might be sent in
their second year, and while not neglecting their mother
tongue, acquire a free use of Latin and Greek in conversation, during their play and at their meals. He
supported his scheme by the success which had attended
this method in the case of Montaigne, who when six
years old could speak Latin better than his native
French. On the other hand, Melanchthon, the restorer
of letters in Germany, and an ardent school reformer
(*Praeceptor Germaniae*, as he was called), strongly
advocates grammatical instruction, and inveighs
vehemently against those who would propose to teach
by practice alone without syntactical precepts. He
calls this method a confused kind of procedure, by
which it is not possible to obtain sound learning. He
considers that those who counsel such a method are
the worst friends of youth, and that they recommend
what is not only pernicious in its effects while the pupils
are still boys, but hurtful to them throughout life. A
contempt for grammatical precepts will engender a
similar contempt for the groundwork of other arts,
and sap the foundations of that reverence which is
the support of private and public morals. He con-

L

siders that 'penalties ought to be inflicted by the State on those teachers who despise grammatical rules.'

The eminent Lipsius deplores the years, from ten to thirteen, which he spent over grammatical trifles, and thinks that the time would be better spent in reading, and in obtaining a knowledge of things. Caselius also advocated the reading of authors, and constant exercises in writing Latin. Ratich, Comenius's distinguished predecessor in the work of Educational Reform, was of Caselius's opinion, but his method was to put an author level with a boy's capacity into a pupil's hands at once—such an author as Terence—to get him to read and re-read the Latin, in the expectation that with some explanation by the master he would begin gradually to understand. At the third reading only should exercises in declining and conjugating be given, and this not in accordance with rules, but merely referring from time to time to types of declensions and conjugations. At the fourth reading the syntax and phraseology generally should be taken up and taught by the master, but all from the author himself. The master according to this method does almost everything, the pupils being to a great extent passive. Ratich had many followers, and some keen opponents.

Lubinus desired some compendious way, and advocated the construction of a book containing pictures of things, with a certain number of brief sentences attached to each, till all the words and phrases of Latin were exhausted. These, he said, should be explained in order, and committed to memory.

But the most important attempt, in Comenius's opinion (as I have elsewhere stated), was that made by an Irishman—a Jesuit father in the Anglican seminary at Salamanca, to which reference has been already made. This man, in conversation with some Englishmen, members of an embassy to Spain, when asked how a man might learn the Spanish language quickly, commended his own method for learning Latin. He had printed a book in which Latin words with a Spanish translation were arranged in complete sentences, in such a way (the same words never being repeated) that any one learning these sentences would know the foundations of the Latin tongue. This conversation took place in 1605, and the book itself was afterwards published in England with an English and French version, and was reproduced in Germany with the addition of a German version by Isaac Habrecht. The celebrated Scioppius published a Latin-Italian edition, and afterwards, in 1636, at Basel, an edition in Latin-German-Greek-Hebrew appeared.

In 1628, says Comenius, when meditating on the subject of a Latin first book, and having already come to the conclusion that words and things were best learned together, 'I planned a book in which all things, the properties of things, and actions and passions of things, should be presented, and to each should be assigned its own proper word, believing that in one and the same book the whole connected series of things might be surveyed historically, and the whole fabric of things and words reduced to one continuous context. On mentioning my purpose to some friends, one of them directed my attention to the Jesuit father's *Janua Linguarum*, and gave me a copy. I leapt with joy ; but on examination, I found that it did not fulfil my plan.

In 1631 Comenius issued his *Janua Lingua Latinae Reserata*, which was cordially received, and found its way by translation into most European, and some Asiatic, languages. A short experience of the book satisfied him that an introduction to it was needed, and he then published a *Vestibulum* in 1632. The idea and plan of the *Palatium* and *Thesaurus*[1] (as mentioned in the *Didactica*) followed in due course.

THE METHOD.

It appears that many teachers, believing that there was some hidden virtue in the *Janua* of Comenius, had used it without discretion, and had consequently been disappointed in the results. Comenius points out that while a good text-book is always essential to the teacher, the expected fruits can be gathered only by the application of a good method.

The desideratum which method supplies is a simple and short way to the knowledge of a language. So far as words are concerned, this way is through things. Words are only the ministers of things, and if we study the former through the latter, we shall find one of the first conditions of good method satisfied. Hence the

[1] Called sometimes *Atrium* and *Palatium.*

text-books published by Comenius which have been so frequently referred to, and which will be described in our next chapter.

But this is not all: the teacher must not only see that the pre-conditions of a good method are satisfied; but he must himself follow a sound method in teaching. What is that method? It is already laid down in the *Great Didactic* syncretically, *i.e.* worked out by comparison with something else, viz., Nature. But Comenius, never weary of his task, takes up the question afresh, and now deals with it analytically. He asks the question, 'What is it to teach?' and answers, 'To make another learn and know what the teacher already knows.' To do this with art, is to follow certain defined paths in teaching which will insure that acquisition is quick, easy, and solid. He then asks 'what it is to learn,' and answers, 'To advance to the knowledge of the unknown through the known.' From this analytic statement he deduces, under the head of General Didactic, eighty propositions in thoroughly scholastic style, and with not a little of the scholastic poverty of genuine substance. It would be a waste of time to go through these in detail, as all that is really valuable has been already exhibited in the *Great Didactic.* Some of his propositions, however, are worth quoting:—

Where nothing is taught, nothing is learned.

Where the teaching is confused, the learning is confused.

Where the teaching is negligent, the learning is negligent.

Do not begin to teach any one who is unprepared for the teaching.

Do not put off teaching one who is prepared.

Labour is for the learner; for the teacher, direction of the learners.

All things are to be taught by the threefold way of Examples, Precepts, and Exercises.

Let the example always come first, the precept next, and let the imitation by way of exercise follow close.

Let rules be short, clear, and true.

Discipline is the means used to press on learning.

Without discipline nothing is learned, or at least nothing rightly.

Discipline must be a never-ceasing constant pressure; never violent; and always graduated, so as to be fitted to its end, corporal chastisement being the final resort.

To learn is easier than to unlearn.

To teach is easier than to unteach, for the latter is a double process, the former a single one.

In teaching we have to advance from few things to many, from the brief to the more lengthened, from the simple to the complex, from the general to the special, from the near to the remote, from the regular to the irregular.

Comenius passes from General Didactic to Special Didactic, applying the general principles which he has laid down to the method of instruction in Science (which is knowledge generally), in Arts, and finally, in Language, and to the general improvement of schools, traversing necessarily much of the ground already traversed in the *Great Didactic.*

In dealing with Science, he gives prominence to the dictum, *Nihil est in intellectu quod non prius in sensu.* The senses are the primary and the constant guides of knowledge. They are the sole solid foundations of knowledge. Wherever it is possible, therefore, all teaching should refer back to this ultimate basis of sense. We must see that the thing represented is understood. To know the differences of things is to know things.

As to Memory: To this there is necessary, first, a clear, firm, and true impression on the senses; secondly, the understanding of what is presented. Words by themselves, if capable of no order or coherence that can engage the understanding, are not to be committed to memory, *e.g.* the vocables *anima, esse, res, ordo,* difficult to remember if so learned, are easily remembered thus, *Ordo est anima rerum.* Writing is a great aid to memory. *Repetitio memoriae pater et mater est.*

Comenius, when he comes to Language, explains that it is more difficult to acquire language than to learn any one department of knowledge or science; and this because it is co-extensive with all knowable things. Here he gives some preliminary directions: *e.g.*—

The teacher is not to teach as much as he is competent to teach, but only as much as the learner can take in.

Examples rather than precepts or rules are to be preferred in the earlier stages of teaching.

The teacher has to exercise patience, as everything must go slowly with beginners.

A teacher who is learned in his department, and of quick parts, is apt to lose his temper : he should remember that his business is not to transform minds, but to inform them.

The questions of the *Great Didactic* are now repeated :—How is language to be learnt quickly, pleasantly, solidly? And the general answer is, Quickly, by constant familiarising with examples ; pleasantly, by giving clear precepts ; solidly, by continual practice ; and all these objects are attained generally by following good method. That is to say :—

To insure Quickness.—Clearly lay down the end at which you aim, and neglect all that does not bear on that end : keep to one example and one explanation of it, relying on practice for all else : advance by gradual steps, never *per saltum :* remember that steady, continuous progress is notable progress ; therefore, no day without a line, no hour without its task : leave nothing undone when once begun.

To insure Pleasantness.—The secret of a pleasant process lies in the handling of the minds of the young in accordance with nature. To do otherwise is to struggle against nature. Everything should be done with paternal affection, all moroseness being banished. Brevity, order, definiteness, should characterise the substance of our teaching. The senses must be always appealed to when possible. As human nature rejoices in *doing*, everything should be learned through its own praxis. The utility and bearing of what is learned should be made manifest. Teaching should be tempered with an agreeable variety, and the playful element admitted. The rivalry and emulation of free games should be encouraged in lessons: *Quidquid in ludo literario, lusus ingenii sit.*

To insure Solidity.—The leading principle here is that we teach the young solid truth, and what will be of solid use, avoiding frivolous things, and indeed everything the truth and utility of which are not patent. Let our examples be very select, placing the thing to be learned distinctly before the eyes, so that every part of it be seen: let the rules be few, brief, clear: let exercises be appended sufficient in number to bring the example and rule clearly out, as without these a vague idea leads to vague and uncertain imitation. Let the first foundations be solidly laid; the beginnings of things are the most important; they should be taught slowly and accurately. By precipitancy everything is destroyed. Let everything therefore be rightly apprehended in its beginning, and secure this by examination. The foundations being solidly laid, proceed cautiously with the superstructure. Let nothing be laid on the top of foundations not yet firmly settled. *Non multa sed multum.* Those who sow much and plough little, lose much and reap little. *Minus serere et melius arare satius est.* Bring all the senses into requisition wherever possible. Above all, the examples and rules being given, give continual practice. Let repetitions and examinations be constant. Let the pupils be required to teach what they have acquired. Comenius presses the great importance of this: *Tanto quis erit doctior, quanto docuerit frequentius.* Fortius says, *Multa ego didici a preceptoribus meis, sed plura a condiscipulis meis; a discipulis autem plurima.*

Comenius continues to enforce these principles, especially pressing the importance of graded books with only as much of the grammar or formal part of language as is necessary to the understanding of them, and with suitable lexicons attached. He points out the importance of giving the pupil root-words and the formation of their derivatives so as to give a stock of vocables. He recurs frequently to the proposition, which with him is vital, that a language is to be learned through things, and that the text which treats of things shall be the source out of which all language-knowledge shall be drawn; the grammar and lexicon, even in their graded and modified forms, being merely subsidiary. This leads him to the description of the principles on which his own school-books were constructed.

Without books artificially constructed it is evident that Comenius's method could not be carried out: these books present, according to him, a sure, short, and pleasant mode of access to all Latin authors. The same things are treated of in each, but at each successive stage in more advanced form—the *Vestibulum* giving only the simplest sentences, comprising primitive and root-words, and only the ordinary regular inflections and rules; the *Janua* introducing to the full grammatical structure and body of the language, and the *Atrium* introducing to phrases, idioms, and elegances; all these taken together constituting, as the initial letters of these various books indicate, a *Via* to authors. The best instruments, however, are useless without a good method of teaching, and a teacher who is not only skilled in his art, but 'greedy of teaching:' if any other shall take up the work, he will prostitute both himself and his art.

Following the above method, and using text-books such as those compiled by the author, the pupil is brought within the Palace of Latin Authors. He has been already furnished with all the words necessary to enable him to enter with advantage on the study of those which treat of *Realia*, such as Pliny in Natural Science, Vitruvius in Architecture; in Medicine, Celsus; in Economics, Varro and Columella, etc. But with a view to phrases and the daily forms of speech, and oratorical and poetical language, he must study other authors, or rather portions of them. For this, the first requirement is a lexicon. Again, whatever author is read, the Grammar should never be absent: if the author is in one hand, the Grammar should be in the other, as Erasmus recommends.

To acquire a thorough knowledge of Latin, and the power of writing it purely and elegantly, the method is threefold, viz., by *Analysis*, by *Excerpts*, and by *Imitation.*

1. *Analysis.*—The object of this is accurate translation into the vernacular. First, by close attention ascertain the purport of the passage before you; then

examine closely the way in which the author attains his end, what words he uses, what phrases, what arguments, what sentences, how these are arranged, until you have, as it were, rearticulated the text. Superficial study is of little value.

2. *Excerption.*—Transfer into a repertory or diary all words, phrases, and opinions, etc., which strike you.

3. *Imitation.*—This has three stages. *First*, Metaphrasis, *i.e.* turning an author into the vernacular, and after some days retranslating him into Latin, comparing the result with the original, and making the requisite corrections. *Secondly*, Turning the Latin into Latin, thus : take the words in confused order, and try to write them correctly ; or, abridge the text ; or, amplify it by the insertion of additional words in the form of epithets, phrases, or sentences. *Thirdly*, Imitation proper : attempt, in the form of a familiar epistle or otherwise, to write in the style of the author who has been selected for imitation, on a subject of present importance but similar to that treated of by the Latin author, comparing our production with that of the classic selected for imitation, until we have so transformed ourselves into him, *e.g.* Cicero, that nothing will be agreeable to our ears which has not a Ciceronian sound.

In following these practical directions we must take care to keep to *one* author as our model, and to practise daily. The exercises should also be graduated in difficulty : in retranslating into Latin, for example, the work should at first be done immediately after reading the passage, and, after a little practice, at longer intervals.

With a view to promote the universal and ready acquisition of Latin, Comenius again suggests, as part of his method, the institution of schools which would be 'Roman cities,' and where nothing but Latin should be spoken or heard.

He further points out how, by the adoption of his method, the learning of many languages would be facilitated, for not only would the same method be followed, but the same sequence of initiatory books in a parallel series. The Grammars of the various languages also would be constructed on the same lines as the Latin grammar in so far as the languages were common.

After showing that the method of studying language is applicable, *mutatis mutandis*, to all arts and sciences, and recommending the construction of systematic compendiums of all things on the ascending scale of his Latin text-books (*e.g.* in Philosophy a *Vestibulum*, then a *Janua*, and then an *Atrium*), Comenius proceeds to show the influence which his method would exercise in improving the internal condition of schools, in promoting learning and a genuine, thorough, and widespread acquisition of the Latin tongue, in attracting the learned to the study of things instead of words, and concludes with an appeal to theologians and to the secular powers.

———————

PART III.

COMENIUS'S TEXT-BOOKS AND THE WAY OF USING THEM.

In the writing of text-books Comenius had his predecessors. The method of Lubinus, which I have briefly explained on page 162, approximates very closely to that of Comenius, while the *Janua* of the Jesuit father must have supplied a valuable repertory of words and phrases.

It is to mistake Comenius's plan to say that his object was to arrange all the more common words of the Latin tongue in a series of sentences, with a view to exhaust all the ordinary vocabulary. He wishes to attain this end certainly, but through *things*. He considers that if he can conceive a course of elementary lessons on *things* in general, he will necessarily call into requisition all the usual vocabulary of Latin, and so teach Latin through things. This is in accordance with his great pansophic idea.

1. THE VESTIBULUM.

First Edition.

This *Latin Primer*, though published subsequently to the *Janua*, comes first in order. It is an introduction to the *Janua*, and, for this reason, Comenius departed from his first intention of making it a series of simple colloquies. Upwards of 1000 Latin words were selected and reduced to short sentences, all of them dealing with things and their properties. These were thrown into seven chapters comprising 427 sentences. The chapters are thus entitled :—

1. *Concerning the accidents or qualities of things ;* no verbs being used save the substantive verb, *e.g.* 'Deus est aeternus; mundus temporarius. Color est multiplex: creta alba, tabula nigra, cinnabaris rubra. Mel est dulce, sal salsum. Ossa dura, caro mollis, glacies lubrica,' and so forth over sixty-two propositions.

2. *Concerning the actions and passions of things—e.g.* 'Sol lucet, luna splendet, stellae micant. Ignis ardet, flamma flagrat. Herba crescit, folium viret, flos floret.' In this way he runs through the most obvious facts concerning things in the heavens; the elements; man's body (*e.g.* caput repletur cerebro, tegiturque capillis, excepto vultu); the mind, diseased conditions, the different trades, etc.

3. *The third chapter treats of the circumstances of things*, and this enables the author to introduce adverbs, prepositions, and numerals. For example : 'Ubi fuisti? unde redis? Ex oppido. Cum nobis ducimus, ante nos pellimus, a nobis trudimus.'

4. *The fourth chapter treats of things in the school.* For example : 'Atramentum est in atramentario : calami in calamario; quibus scribimus in charta,' etc.

5. *The fifth chapter treats of things at home.*

6. *Concerning things in the city.*

7. *Concerning the Virtues.*

The rule followed is the opposite of that now almost universal in elementary books; words are never repeated if it be possible to avoid repetition.

The German is given in parallel columns, and the pupil is required to read the German first, and then the Latin. The lesson said in the morning is always to be written in the afternoon. After going several times through the book, the pupil learns it off by heart, so many sentences each day. Along with the reading, the declension and conjugation of the words proceeds: first, nouns by themselves, then nouns with adjectives. Tables of the declensions and conjugations are appended, to which reference is constantly to be made. In declining, the terminations of the cases are not to be said by heart, but to be first learned by practice, the teacher giving the vernacular first, *e.g. nubès*—what is *of* a cloud? what is *to* or *for* a cloud? and so on, the boy referring to his tables. After this has been done several times, the tables are quickly and easily committed to memory. Thus the boy who has properly mastered this Latin Primer will have acquired 1000 vocables, and a knowledge of the regular declensions and conjugations.

In the *Dissertatio de sermonis Latini studio* he enters even more into detail; the *Vestibulum*, he says, is first to be read and written out for the sake of the Latin words only, without translation. The pupil is then to begin it over again and translate, first, the vernacular into the Latin, and thereafter the Latin into the vernacular.

Some knowledge of the parts of speech is to be obtained, but parsing is not to be pressed. The chief things are the easy reading and writing, and the thorough acquisition of the words. The vernacular version is to be prefixed to each separate sentence (later the author was content with a vernacular version printed by itself, but as one book with the Latin). In all cases the vernacular is to be first learned. The index at the end of the *Vestibulum* is to be used in this way: a word is to be given, and the sentence, or series of words in the text where it is found, is then to be given by the pupil from memory. The writing of the morning's lessons at the afternoon meetings is constantly insisted on by Comenius, because this exercise, by engaging the senses, fixes the exercise in the minds of the pupils. The learning of the tables of declensions is to be begun only at the fourth reading of the text-book. Comenius assumes that the text-book will be perused ten times, and in this way thoroughly got by heart. Before leaving it, exercises were to be given in translating into Latin fresh sentences more or less connected, composed of the words in the *Vestibulum* and its index.

Second Edition.

I have been thus particular in describing the first edition of the *Vestibulum*, and the mode of using it, because all the principles of Comenius's method of procedure are exemplified in it, in so far as these can be embodied in a text-book, and because it exhibits the plan of his other books.

M

In the second edition of the *Vestibulum* (published, or at least written, between 1650 and 1654, during his school experience in Hungary) the plan is altered. Comenius had made up his mind that, as children, when learning to speak, used words before they made sentences, so the *Vestibulum* should consist of lists of words only, with this condition, that there should be a coherence between the words of a group, thus :—

57. *Elementa*—Ignis, aer, aqua, terra.
58. In aethere—Sidera.
    A quibus veniunt—Calor, frigus, aestus, gelu.
59. Sidera sunt—Sol, luna, stella.
60. In sole sunt—Lux, radius, lumen.
    Sine lumine est—Umbra, caligo, tenebrae.
61. Ab igne venit—Flamma, scintilla, fumus, et fuligo.

And so on, selecting associated words, and, as much as possible, primitive words, under 500 classes of *things*. The words are in number about 5000. The boy who had got up the whole thoroughly would accordingly possess some 5000 vocables, besides the outlines of Latin accidence. A broader basis was thus laid for that encyclopædic knowledge of things, and of words through things, than could otherwise be done.[1]

Mode of using the Vestibulum.—The object is to prepare for the *Janua*. The class using the book must be able to write fluently, as well as to read articulately,

---

[1] We get hints as to the use of this Latin Primer from Comenius's letter to the teacher of the Vestibulary class at Patak, also from the *De Vestibulari Praxi*, etc.

Latin words, whether in print or MS. They will learn by heart the words of the Latin tongue given in their text-book, with the translation of them, and acquire perfect familiarity with the regular declensions and conjugations. The vernacular of the Latin is to be prefixed to the school editions of the book, and this is to be first read and learned, and thereafter the Latin. In this way the words, which introduce to the elements of encyclopædic knowledge, will be first known in their relation to things, and then the Latin words in relation to the vernacular, the pupil thus going from the known to the unknown. Two months should be spent in thoroughly understanding and acquiring the vernacular text, in fact in learning it by heart, before entering on the Latin equivalent. The Latin text is then to occupy four months. The teacher is always to read and explain beforehand what his pupils are afterwards to read and explain, and to be careful that no lesson is passed from till it is thoroughly acquired. The pupils are then to write the exercise in a book, and to conclude with saying it by heart. The outlines of Latin grammar are given in Latin, but they are to be carefully translated and understood before being learned. Three months are presumed to suffice for learning the grammar. The directions given have simply reference to the thorough acquisition of the forms. They are to be learned by heart, but above all, questions are to be asked in every possible way, and these questions are to be put in Latin. Little sentences are to be constructed illustrating the cases, tenses, etc. etc., and after all this is done the text of the *Vestibulum* is to be again gone over and parsed. The Lexicon, which is simply a list of words with number-references to the part of the text in which they may be found, is finally to be read over—chiefly to test the pupil's knowledge of the meaning of all the words he is presumed now to have acquired.

In his *Ventilabrum Sapientiae* he expresses a desire that the *Vestibulum* should be thrown into a dialogue form, that the vernacular of the Latin rules should be printed in parallel columns, and that pictures of the things named should be introduced.

In 1657 Comenius published an addition to the last edition of the *Vestibulum*, in which the primitive words already used, and many others, were worked up into short simple sentences. This book (called the *Auctarium*) was intended to serve as a revision of the work done in the *Vestibulum*, to initiate into the construction of sentences, and to serve as a bridge to the *Janua*. But it was distinguished from the *Vestibulum* in this respect, that whereas the latter was an arrangement of words under the head of Things (classified), the former was alphabetically arranged—was in fact a lexicon thrown into simple sentences—*e.g.* under *B* we have such sentences as these : Baccas fert laurus, non betula, vel butus. Bellua maxima, in sylvis est Barrus, in aquis balaena ; and so forth. The title of the book was *Parvulis parvulus, omnibus omnia. Hoc est, Vestibuli Latinae linguae Auctarium; voces Latinas primitivas construi coeptas et in sententiolas breves redactas exhibens.*

In praeludium Sylvam Latinam ingressuris datam, i.e. 'A little book for little ones, all things for all : that is to say, a Supplement to the Vestibule of the Latin tongue, exhibiting Latin primitive words in construction, and thrown into brief little sentences, given as a prelude to those about to enter the Latin Forest'—the 'Forest' being the collection of Latin words which formed the introduction to the last edition of the *Janua.*

An accident led him to construct the *Auctarium.* When in Amsterdam in 1656 he had his attention directed to an edition of the *Janua,* published in England with additions—those additions professing to give the roots of the Latin tongue woven into sentences. He found that this addition departed in almost every respect from the principles of his books, and was of a kind to disgust rather than to attract boys. The idea, however, pleased him, and he set himself to construct the supplement to the *Vestibulum* under the title above given. It is to be used as a revisal of the *Vestibulum* and a bridge to the *Janua.* It was published in 1657.

2. The Janua Linguae Latinae reserata.
First Edition.

The full title of this famous book is *The Gate of Languages Unlocked, or the Seminary of all Languages and Sciences:* that is, a compendious method of learning Latin or any other tongue, along with the elements of all the Sciences and Arts, comprehended under a hundred chapter-headings and in a thousand sentences; first published in the year 1631.

The one thousand sentences again comprehend eight thousand different words in all. The sentences are at first simple, and thereafter compound and complex. After an introduction he begins, according to his pansophic or encyclopædic plan, with the origin of the world, and in the course of his lessons takes a survey of all nature, and even includes morals and religion. It frequently happens, however, that a chapter is introduced for the sake of the *words*, not of the things taught: for example, the chapter on Ulcers and Wounds. The easiest sentences are of this fashion, 'Deus omnia creavit ex nihilo.' The more difficult are exemplified by the following, 'Incendium ex quavis scintilla, si permittis, oritur. Nam quidquid ignem concipit, id primum gliscit, dein ardet, tum flagrat et flammat; postremo, crematum redigitur in favillas et cineres.'

Carrying out his expressed aim, Comenius endeavours throughout to give equal attention to both things and words, but it is *things* that give the cue. The headings of some of his chapters will convey some idea of the scope of his writing:—Concerning the Origin of the World. Concerning the Elements. Concerning the Firmament, Fire, Meteors, Waters, Earths, Stones, Metals, Trees and Fruits, Herbs, Shrubs. These things are treated of in thirteen chapters and one hundred and forty-one sentences. Then we have 'Concerning Animals,' which, under different subdivisions, occupies the book to the nineteenth chapter inclusive. Then Concerning Man: his Body; External Members; Internal Members; the qualities or accidents of the Body; Diseases; Ulcers and Wounds; the External Senses; the Internal Senses; Mind; the Will and the Affections: these occupy the book to the twenty-ninth chapter inclusive. All the mechanic arts now follow, and are concluded in the forty-eighth chapter and 539th sentence. The rest of the book treats of the House and its parts: Marriage and the Family, in which occur statements which are very curious as showing the freedom with which things were spoken about to the young of 250 years ago. Next follows Civic and State Economy, including a description of officers and institutions. The seventieth chapter begins with Grammar, and goes on to Dialectic, Rhetoric, Arithmetic, Geometry, and all branches of knowledge, briefly describing what these are. In the eighty-second chapter Ethics is introduced, and twelve chapters are assigned to twelve virtues. Games, Death, Burial, the Providence of God and Angels form the subjects of the concluding chapters. This is encyclopædism.

The German equivalent ran in parallel columns, and was to be read first.

Comenius thus, with great labour and no small ingenuity, gives effect to his own conceptions of the substance of school-instruction and the method of teaching languages at one and the same time. The reader will at once see that the lines on which the *Janua* are constructed are precisely the same as those on which the *Vestibulum* is laid down, and the following higher-class text-book (*Atrium*) again repeats (as will shortly be seen) the substance of the *Janua* in a still more developed and extended form. A brief grammatical Appendix and Lexicon was to be added to the *Janua*, but I have not met with these except in connection with the new edition, of which I will now speak.

Second Edition.

The improved form of the *Janua* was published between 1650-54, during his school experience in Hungary, though substantially written at Elbing before 1650. It is on the same lines as the first edition, but much more elaborate and more difficult. In the fifteenth chapter of the *Novissima Linguarum Methodus* he partly explains the changes made. He has discarded the restriction he had previously imposed on himself, of not repeating words : this he calls a superstition. The greater latitude thus allowed enables him to write about 'things' more fully and freely. The Lexicon, or Forest of Words (*Sylva Verborum*), strange to say (and contrary to his original plan),[1] comes first, and aims at being etymological throughout. Moreover, it is Latin-Latin and not Latin-vernacular. He intends this Lexicon to be first gone over, then the Grammar which follows, and finally the *Janua* itself. As to a vernacular-Latin Lexicon, he thinks that boys should construct that for themselves. Again, whereas it was thought desirable that the vernacular should accompany, nay precede, the

---

[1] But in accordance with the plan of the second edition of the *Vestibulum.*

Latin in the original *Janua*, the former is now discarded. The reasons for beginning with the Lexicon, and then proceeding to the Grammar and thereafter to the text of the *Janua*, curiously illustrate the fancifulness of the author's mind. 'When we want to build a [wooden] house we first go to the wood and cut down trees (this is the Lexicon of words); then we shape and fit the wood cut down (this is the Grammar); and it is only then we proceed to build the house (*i.e.* to give continuous narrative).' The practical result is that the pupil has to go through lists of vocables which would fill two hundred octavo pages, and then a Grammar which would fill fifty, before he begins the text-book itself. The text itself is composed of one hundred short treatises about everything on the earth, in the earth, and above the earth, including an account of man, and brief statements of morals and theology. It is, in short, an encyclopædia, arranged not alphabetically, but in a natural order, and would fill 250 pages of an ordinary school-book. Comenius apologises, indeed, for not introducing everything about everything; the state of knowledge, he regrets, does not admit of it. The vocables of the Lexicon are not by any means exhausted in the text, but all the words in the text are understood to be found in the Lexicon; but when the boy finds them there, which he very often will not, he is presented with their significations in Latin only !

I shall give here a specimen of his lessons, taking the beginning of his eighteenth lesson.

Quadrupeda: primum, mansueta pecora et jumenta.

Quadrupes quid, 161 : partes illius essentiales, 162 : genera, 163: pecora majora, 164: et minora, 165, 6, 7, 8: jumenta, 169 : Canes, feles, mures, 170, 71, 72.

161. Quadrupeda progenerant foetum vivum, aluntque lacte uberum : grandiora unicum et rarius, minutiora plures et frequentius.

162. Pro integumento habent vel pilos vel villos vel lanam vel setas vel squamas ; pedes autem vel digitatos armatos unguibus (ut Canis, etc.,) vel ungulatos: et quidem ungulave solida (ut equus) vel bifida (ut bos).

And so on through twelve paragraphs.

It is quite clear that Comenius, under the influence of some fantastic notions of consistency developed in his *Novissima Methodus*, has deserted nearly all that is most characteristic and original in his system, excepting his encyclopædism. Of this he never loses sight.

Mode of using the Janua.[1]—The Lexicon, or words, come first, then the Grammar, which teaches how to weave these words into speech, and then the text of the *Janua*, which lays the foundations, in a series of lessons, of all knowledge. Comenius defends this order, as I have said, on the ground that words are the rudiments of speech, and that the materials of house-building must be supplied before we begin to build a house. The boys accordingly are first to read with the master the words and their derivatives, as set down in the Lexicon,

---

[1] *See* Letter to the Teacher of the Janual Class ; also *De Latini sermonis studio dissertatio*, and elsewhere.

as often as may be necessary, then take their pens and transcribe them into their writing-books, and, finally, say them by heart. The Grammar, which is a complete syntax of the language, omitting elegancies, etc., is, as I have said, Latin, but the prior study of the Lexicon is presumed to make the Latin intelligible, while its simple construction, as compared with other Grammars, makes it easy and attractive. The text of the *Janua* is finally to be taught in the same manner as the *Vestibulum* was taught.

In his later years Comenius himself became sensible of certain defects, and recommended that the vernacular of all words should be given in the Lexicon, and also that the vernacular of the text should be printed in parallel columns; thus returning to his original ideas.

The mode of using the *Janua* is given in more detail in the *Dissertatio de Sermonis Latini Studio, à propos* of the first edition, and he there tells us that the object, as regards mere language, is to give the pupil all the common words of the Latin tongue, to teach him their meanings and roots, and also to teach him to form sentences out of them with grammatical correctness. An Etymological Lexicon and a Grammar containing the *body* of the language (all save special idioms and elegancies) are consequently added.

Like the *Vestibulum*, the *Janua* is to be gone through ten times. At the *second* reading the whole should be written out, vernacular and Latin. The teacher should at this stage speak in Latin to his pupils, and induce them also to speak to each other in Latin; and with a view to the increase of knowledge, will conversationally explain and amplify the lessons of the *Janua*. At the third reading, the teacher will *read out* the Latin and call for the translation. Meanwhile the first part of the Syntactical Grammar will be written out by the pupils. At the fourth perusal, the remainder of the Grammar will be written out, and the naming of the parts of speech and of the inflexions in the text of the *Janua* thoroughly acquired. At the fifth reading, special attention will be given to the roots and derivatives, and the pupils will begin to write out the Lexicon. At the sixth perusal, synonyms, paronyms, etc., will be explained; and at the seventh reading the whole will be thoroughly parsed with reference to the syntactical rules, which will be written out carefully with their subjoined examples. The recitation of the text will begin at the eighth perusal. At the ninth reading special attention will be paid to the logical analysis—examination on the substance of the text and on grammar. This sharpens the wit. The afternoon is always to be spent in writing out the morning's work, in throwing the *Janua* into the form of question and answer. The tenth perusal will consist of the boys challenging each other to repeat parts of the text. The written exercises will consist of Latin compositions, the vernacular being constructed by the teacher (apologues, fables, etc.) out of the words in the *Janua* and its Lexicon, and translated into Latin by the pupils.

It has to be noted that Comenius, in his preface to his *Auctarium* (vol. iv.), distinctly repudiates the first edition of the *Janua*, and wishes to be judged by the second edition, which is substantially a new book. His words are :—' Januam nostram linguarum postremam— pleniorem illam Encyclopaediolae faciem referentem et prae qua priorem illam non amplius agnoscimus nostram.' In doing so he deserted his own principles.

3. THE ATRIUM.

The third Latin book was called the *Atrium*, and this was to effect the transition from the *Janua* to the *Palatium* or *Palace of Authors*.[1] Comenius now wishes to introduce the pupil to the Latin tongue, used in a freer way than in the *Janua*. The sentences are longer, and the treatment of each subject more ample. The main end kept in view is the familiarising of the pupil with the elegancies and idioms of the language, and the introducing him to rhetoric in a practical form. To effect this, he gives a Grammar of Latin specially designed to gather into one view the peculiarities and elegancies of the Latin tongue. This Grammar is written in Latin, and the pupil is to be now presumed competent to understand it. While intent on giving the pupil acquaintance with the varieties and peculiarities of Latin, and furnishing him with a liberal *copia verborum*, he does not depart from his great principle to make things carry words. The text of the *Atrium* follows the same line as the *Janua*, but indulges in a larger and more detailed treatment of the same subjects. In the

---

[1] The *Atrium* is called elsewhere *Palatium* in the *Didactica*, and the *Palatium* is called the *Thesaurus*.

Janua, for example, he contents himself with such a sentence as this :—

'Omnia reliqua ex his [quatuor elementis] constant. Quippe ex iis generantur, iis nutriuntur, in eadem dum corrumpuntur resolvuntur.'

In the *Atrium* he expands this as follows :—

'Hae sunt elementaris mundi rotae quatuor, per quas eunt et redeunt omnia.   Elementis vacans locus nullus est : omnia his referta tamque densé stipata sunt ut inane spatium nusquam detur, sed agitatio, attritus, ·permistio ; quorum temperatura salutem dat rebus, intemperies perniciem.   Solatio est, si quid corrumpitur, in sua redire principia indeque res prodire novas.'

And so on with the usual 100 chapters and 1000 paragraphs (which, in the *Janua*—first edition—were merely short sentences).   In the edition before me, the *Atrium* extends over 153 folio columns, and is considerably longer than Cæsar's *Gallic War.*

The comparison of the two passages which I have cited will give a clear idea of the differences between the two books.

This book having been thoroughly mastered, along with its accompanying Grammar, the pupil is now supposed to be able to enter freely on the study of Latin authors, a *Palatium* or *Thesaurus* of selected works being put before him.   And certainly any boy, who had mastered it, would be quite competent to attack Cæsar, Sallust, and the easier Orations of Cicero.   The poets, however, would present a difficulty, for the reading of whom the way had not been prepared.

Mode of using the Atrium.—A complete Latin Grammar in Latin is prefixed to the *Atrium*, and is to be *first* studied by the pupils ; then the text, and finally the Lexicon. The general method of procedure is presumed to be the same as in the *Janua*, but on this Comenius is not explicit, and it would seem as if he considered the printing of the vernacular to be unnecessary at this advanced stage. We cannot imagine that he intended the *Atrium*, with its Grammar, to be learned by heart. The human mind could not have borne the burden.

SUBSIDIARY TEXT-BOOKS.

1. *The Orbis Pictus* (*The World Illustrated*).

In 1657 appeared the *Orbis Pictus*, the second edition following in 1659. This book was intended to be supplementary and subsidiary to the *Vestibulum* and *Janua*. It is simpler than even the first edition of the *Janua*, and much more suitable for a school-book than the second edition of the *Vestibulum*. In this little book Comenius applies his principles more fully than in any other, for we have not only a simple treatment of things in general, but of things that appeal to the senses, and along with the lessons we have pictures of the objects that form the subjects of the lessons. Indeed, the book may be best described as a series of rude engravings of sensible objects, accompanied by a description of them in short and easy sentences. For example, we have the picture of a ship with its sails partly set, and a number attached to each part of the ship, which corresponds to a number in the lesson — thus: the No. 2 is engraved on the sails, and in the lesson we have this sentence, 'The ship has (2) sails.' The title of the book was, 'The World of Sensible Things drawn; that is, the Nomenclature of all Fundamental Things in the World and Actions in Life reduced to Ocular Demonstration, so that it may be a Lamp to the *Vestibulum* and *Janua* of Languages.'[1]

There were various editions of the *Orbis;* that however which was in most complete accord with Comenius's plan was arranged in three columns, thus:—

Super terra	auf der Erden	terra f.,[1] die Erde.
sunt	sŏnd	
alti montes[1]	hohe berge[1]	altus-a-um, hoch.
profundae valles[2]	tiefe Thäler[2]	profundus-a-um, tief.
Etc.	Etc.	Etc.

The figures referred to a wood-engraving of a landscape on the same page, and were affixed to the mountains, hills, etc., as has been explained above in the case of the lesson on the ship.

'The foundation of all learning consists,' says Comenius in the preface, 'in representing clearly to the senses sensible objects, so that they can be apprehended easily. I maintain that this is the basis of all other actions, inasmuch as we could neither act nor speak wisely unless we comprehended clearly what we wished to say or do. For it is certain that there is nothing in the

[1] In some of the very numerous editions the title is slightly modified. The editions also varied in other respects, but the above gives Comenius's own conception of the book.

Understanding which has not been previously in the Sense; and consequently, to exercise the senses carefully in discriminating the differences of natural objects is to lay the foundation of all wisdom, all eloquence, and all good and prudent action.' It is the absence from the school of the object about which we may be speaking that makes learning and teaching alike so troublesome and fruitless.

The cuts were done by Michael Endter of Nuremberg, to whom he felt most grateful for his labours, and for enabling him to complete his design of an elementary book. 'This work,' he writes, 'belongs to you; it is entirely new in your profession. You have given a correct and clear edition of the *Orbis Pictus*, and furnished figures and cuts, by the help of which the attention will be awakened and the imagination pleased. This will, it is true, increase the expense of the publication, but it will be certainly returned to you.'

It was consistent with the plan of the book, that it should contain the vernacular only, or the Latin only, or both. Comenius suggests that the vernacular itself would be best learned from the *Orbis*. The *Janua* had an enormous sale, and was published in many languages; but the editions and sale of the *Orbis Pictus* far exceeded those of the *Janua*, and, indeed, for some time it was the most popular school-book in Europe, and deservedly so.

N

2. *The Schola Ludus.*

Comenius frequently states in his writings that the element of sport should be introduced into schools, and with this view constructs a school drama, in which the *Janua* (and a good deal of the language of the *Atrium*) is introduced. The title is, *Schola Ludus seu Encyclopaedia Viva, Hoc est, Januae Linguarum praxis Scenica: res omnes nomenclaturâ Vestitas et Vestiendas, sensibus ad vivum repraesentandi artificium exhibens amoenum.* In this singular production there are five acts, twenty-one scenes, and fifty-two *dramatis personae.* The object of the author is to give a theatric praxis of the *Janua,* and partially of the *Atrium,* by bringing the facts of the natural world into a scenic representation. The characters represent the various departments of knowledge, *e.g.* the geographer, the metallurgist, the chemist, and so forth. For example, in the fifth scene of the second act, Water is the subject, and there enter on the stage the following personages :—*Aquinus* (representing water in general), *Marius* (representing the sea) *Nubianus* (representing the clouds), and *Stillico* (representing rain-drops, ice, foam, etc.). These interesting characters give a great deal of valuable information. Anything more dreary than this sportive *Janua* it is impossible to conceive; yet he assures us, in his dedicatory epistle, written at Amsterdam in 1657, that it was most popular and successful with boys and masters! and elsewhere he says that it was performed with great applause before the Princess and all her Court in

Hungary. He believed that all school-exercises might be converted into games.

Comenius was of opinion that every stage of school-work during the Pansophic septennium might have its dramatic exhibition. This dramatic sport in intellectual work he connects mystically with the words of Wisdom (the Son), in the 8th chapter of Proverbs : ' I was by Him as one brought up with Him ; and I was daily His delight, rejoicing always before Him ; rejoicing in the habitable part of His earth; and my delights were with the sons of men !'

The signification of *Ludus* as the Latin for school had also its influence in suggesting these dramatic exhibitions.[1]

3. *Text-Book of Greek.*

He gives a specimen of what he would propose for boys learning Greek in his *Ventilabrum Sapientiae* published in 1657. It is, as might be expected, Latin-Greek. He proposes that Vocabularies should be taught to begin with—1. The words that are alike in Latin and Greek, *e.g.* Abyssus, ἄβυσσος. 2. Those which differ very little, *e.g.* fama, φήμη, forma, μορφή. 3. The more common words not alike, *e.g.* frater, ἀδελφὸς. Then a few brief Greek rules should be given, and an outline of Greek accidence appended to the body of the book. As his chief object was to introduce to the Greek Testament, the text-book, he

---

[1] For the *Palatium*, see end of next chapter.

says, ought to consist of 100 select sentences of a moral
kind (the Latin and Greek in parallel columns), to be
thoroughly learned, the Lord's Prayer, the Creed, and
the Ten Commandments. This would constitute a
Vestibulum, to be followed by a Janua, consisting of the
Greek Testament in Latin and Greek, or it might be a
summary of Testament narrative and of the Christian
faith.

So with Hebrew.

In concluding this account of the text-books, it has
to be stated that Comenius himself in his old age
admitted that he had departed from one of his own
leading principles in attempting to teach too much
within a limited space and time, and had burdened the
mind of boys with what was suitable only for adults.[1]

---

[1] A knowledge of the Text-Books is best to be obtained from
the books themselves, but in connection with them the prefaces
should be read, and the letters addressed to the teachers of the
new Patak School, an account of which is contained in the next
chapter.

PART IV.

PART IV.

THE INNER ORGANISATION OF A PANSOPHIC SCHOOL, AND THE INSTRUCTION-PLAN.

THE external organisation of a school-system has been exhibited in the *Great Didactic*. The Mother School, the Vernacular School, the Latin School or Gymnasium, and the University, constituted together Comenius's school-system for a State. The existing school-systems of modern Europe, and especially that of Germany, are a tribute to Comenius's sound judgment. The organisation of instruction is certainly not in accordance with Comenius's pansophic or encyclopædic aspirations, but the attention which is now given to real studies, and to the cultivation of the senses, substantially give effect to his views.

The inner character and life of a school—a Latin school or Gymnasium being kept specially in view—is to be gathered from the 25th chapter of the *Novissima Methodus*, and from the numerous writings of the period from 1650-54, when Comenius was engaged in organising a model school at Patak, in the north-east of Hungary, about twenty miles from Tokay.[1] These

[1] On the Theiss, known as the entrepôt of the Tokay wine.

writings are numerous, prolix, and very tiresome because of their repetitions. The following account is based on an examination of all these writings, and ought to be compared with the ideas of the various graded schools expounded in the 'Great Didactic.'

THE SCHOOL.

The word school, *schola* or *ludus*, indicates an institution where many are assembled together to strive for some end, but to strive under the conditions of play, and these conditions are movement, spontaneity, society, rivalry, order, and pleasurable exercise, all of which things are to be attained by following the methods laid down. The school will thus truly become a *ludus literarius*. The object of the school as a prelude of life is to train pupils to know with a view to wisdom, to act, to express themselves,—*sapere, agere, loqui.* The letters of the words themselves yield the aims of the school, thus :—

> Sapienter
> Cogitare :
> Honesté
> Operari :
> Loqui
> Arguté.

The initial letters, it will be observed, make the word *Schola*, and this quite suits Comenius's fanciful way of looking at things, and evidently yields him a real satisfaction. The foundation of all is Knowledge, because to act wisely or speak well is impossible for an ignorant or foolish person.

A school has been called *Officina Humanitatis*, a manufactory of humanity, and this designation, as appears from the Great Didactic, Comenius adopts.

Now, when we say that the school is a manufactory of *Humanity*, we mean that it has to aim at producing in men that perfection of humanity whereby a man becomes the image of God, the most Wise, most Powerful, most Holy.

When we say that the school is an *Officina*, we mean that it is a place where, by the use of certain instruments and a certain art, we accomplish what we desire to accomplish. The instruments are the persons and things employed in teaching and learning, and the art is the method laid down whereby tongue, action, hand, and morals become what we desire them to become.

These generally are the aims and characteristics of a school when we have passed within its walls. While keeping them carefully in view, we have to lay down our scheme more fully.

General Statement.

The aim is pansophic or encyclopædic. We have to teach all things to all, if we would train to knowledge and wisdom. We have to instruct in morality and train to virtue; we have to instil piety and train to a pious habit; and, finally, we have to form the tongue to expression and eloquence. Only in this way can we train man to true humanity, and make him again the image of God.

With this view the school must be organised, and a set amount of work marked out for each grade or class. There should be seven classes (those in the lowest class being about twelve years of age). The three lowest classes should be called Philological; the fourth, Philosophical; the fifth, Logical; the sixth, Political; and the seventh, Theological.

The Philological classes would naturally be designated by the text-books they used : the first or lowest, which would use the *Vestibulum*, being called *Classis Vestibularis*, the second *Classis Janualis*, and the third *Classis Atrialis*. The Philosophical class would give a rational account of things ; the Logical would give discipline in reasoning ; the Political would give instruction in laws and the social order (including history) ; and the Theological would instruct in the mysteries of the Kingdom of Heaven.

A separate room and a separate master should be provided for each class, and the building should be on an ample scale. There should be a public table for poor scholars, so that the *res angusta domi* should be an obstacle to none.

In a school so organised, and with such aims, the pupils will learn all things necessary for this life and the next, and that thoroughly. It will be a School of Universal Wisdom—in other words, a *Schola Panso-*

phica.[1] 'There is nothing in Heaven or Earth, or in the Waters, nothing in the Abyss under the earth, nothing in the Human Body, nothing in the Soul, nothing in Holy Writ, nothing in the Arts, nothing in Economy, nothing in Polity, nothing in the Church, of which the little candidates of Wisdom shall be wholly ignorant.' They will be trained further in the true and spontaneous use of knowledge, and in prudence and morality. In this *palaestra* they 'will learn, not for school, but for life,' so that the youths shall go forth energetic, ready for everything, apt, industrious, and worthy of being intrusted with any of the duties of life, and this all the more if they have added to virtue a sweet conversation, and have crowned all with the fear and love of God. They will also go forth capable of expression and eloquence, and that not merely in their own tongue, but in the Latin, Greek, and Hebrew.

For the attainment of these great results three instruments are necessary: good books, good teachers, and a good method.

The seven classes into which the school is to be divided are to consist respectively of those pupils who are at the same stage of progress, and are pursuing the same objects of study. Each class should be in a separate room, that the attention of the pupils may not be distracted. Each class, again, should be divided

---

[1] 'Schola Pansophica : Hoc est, Universalis Sapientiae officina ab annis aliquot ubiubigentium erigi optata : nunc autem Auspiciis Illustrissimi Domini *D. Sigismundi Racoci* de Felseovadas, etc. Saros-Pataki Hungarorum feliciter erigenda. Anno redditae mundi salutis MDCLI.'

into decuriae composed of ten boys each, and presided over by a boy older or more advanced than his fellows, who should be called Moderator, Inspector, Pædagogus, or Decurio.   The duty of the decurio will be to see that all the boys of his division are in their places at the right time, that they attend to the work of the moment, to assist backward boys, or report them to the preceptor, and to be an example of conduct to all.   The master himself shall not stand in a corner, nor shall he walk about, but he will occupy a raised position facing the light, so that he may see and be seen by all, and where drawings and illustrations of lessons may also be easily seen.

The school-time must be so ordered that every year, month, week, day, hour, may have its own task.   The tasks should be so arranged that they are within the powers of the average mind : in this way the more ordinary natures will be stimulated, while the more precocious and brilliant will be retarded to their advantage.   Pupils should be admitted only at the beginning of the school year.   On no day should boys do more than six hours' work, and those all in public and in school.   The rest should be given to relaxation and domestic duties.   The school is the proper place for *school* work ; moreover, home-work is apt to be badly done, and badly done work is more hurtful than no work at all.   The hours should not be consecutive : the morning should be devoted to studies that call into requisition the intellect, the judgment, and the memory; the afternoon to the discipline of hand, voice, style, demeanour (*gestus*).

The occupations of the Pansophic school are not all of equal importance. They may be classed as primary, secondary, and tertiary. The primary are those which contain the essence or substance of Wisdom (knowledge), Virtue, Piety, and Eloquence, such as Languages, Philosophy, and Theology; the secondary are auxiliary to these, such as History; the tertiary only indirectly contribute to the primary occupations, *e.g.* all that pertains to vigour of health and mental alacrity, such as recreation and sports. But all the occupations and studies have a place *at each successive stage* of progress, and are to be presented *according to the same method*.

At the same time, the order of the instruction is subject to certain general laws : for in the younger classes we have to appeal chiefly to the senses, and to cultivate observation ; and as the pupils advance, we draw more on the activity of the memory, the intellect proper, and the power of expressing what is known.

In the exercise of these powers there are also degrees : for example, under the head of the Intellect there are three stages ; the first comprehends the statement of fact, the second the why of the fact, and the third the fundamental principles which underlie the fact and its reason, and enable the student to extend his investigations in the same line : for example, a knowledge of the compass and of the use of it is the first stage, a knowledge of its construction and relation to other things is the second stage, and such a knowledge of the principles lying at the foundation of its construction and application as will enable the student to advance further in the same line of investigation is the third stage. So in Language you have three stages : the power to prattle, to speak, and to speak eloquently, and instruction must proceed in this order. The same remarks apply to the graduated order of auxiliary studies, such as History. This word is used in an extended sense : in the third, or Atrial class, it means stories which bear on the daily affairs of life and on morals ; in the fourth, or Philosophical class, it deals with Natural History—the study of the works of God ; in the fifth, or Logical class, it deals with the history of human inventions—mechanical history ; in the sixth, or Political class, it deals with the history of the customs of various nations ; and in the seventh, or Theological class, it deals with the universal history of man in the Providence of God. The first or Vestibulary, and the second or Janual class, are here omitted, because they are occupied with the mere nomenclature of things, which stands for history to young children. The same remarks apply (but are not always successfully applied by Comenius) to all the studies and exercises of the school.

The senses, he has said, have to be specially appealed to in the earliest classes, since they are the guides to knowledge. *We* do not speak to our pupils, but the *things themselves ;* and everything should be taught by means of the things themselves, or where these fail, by accurate representations of them. The walls of the school should be hung with pictures, and the reading-books should be full of them. The intellect again will be exercised by the explanation of everything that is read or taught, and by requiring the explanation to be given by the scholars,—for we do not form parrots, but men. The memory also has to be cultivated, for, as Quintilian says, *Tantum scimus quantum memoria tenemus*. But the exercise of the memory does not mean the wearing the pupil out by requiring him to learn things off by heart; but the frequent and sufficient presentation of things clearly understood, till, of their own accord, they adhere. Weekly memory-contests, at which the pupils challenge each other to state what has been learned, will be of value in stimulating the memory.

As regards style: let the pupils be required to write weekly letters to one another on given subjects, and let the decurio look after these, under the supervision of the master.

The tongue will be exercised by requiring that the conversation of the boys one with another be in Latin. The voice will be cultivated by teaching all to sing, and by teaching notation at certain fixed times.

The morals and demeanour of the pupils will receive the close attention of the masters, and their reproof of wrong, and their commendation of good conduct will always be prompt. Further, the formation of a school, and even of individual classes, into a republic, with its senate and proctor, which will hold sessions occasionally, and pronounce judgment on conduct, will do much to prepare for the business of life.

Piety will be fostered by taking care that in going to bed and rising, prayers be said and the Holy Scriptures read; also in beginning and ending the studies of the day, and before and after meals.

To encourage the more active-minded boys, special reading should be allowed of authors outside the usual school-course, such as the sacred dialogues of Castalio, the Colloquies of Erasmus, Epistles of Seneca, the Histories of Nepos, Curtius, etc.

All sorts of exercises and innocent games are to be not only permitted but encouraged, for giving vigour and health to the body; and also sedentary games which call for a certain quickness of wit.

Scenic representations and the acting of plays are to be encouraged as a relaxation, so long as the subject is not immoral in its character or treatment, as are the Roman plays, but constructed to represent some memorable histories, sacred or profane. These not only afford recreation, but are educationally of good effect in many ways.

The times of relaxation should be frequent—half-an-hour after every hour's work. The daily time-table should be arranged somewhat as follows :—

Forenoon.

6 to 7 A.M.	Hymns, Reading of Scripture, Meditation, and Prayers.
7½—8½	The primary task of the class—more theoretically given.
9—10	The same practically given.

Afternoon.

1—2 P.M.	Music, or some other pleasant mathematical exercise.
2.30—3.30	History.
4—5	Exercises in Style.

There should be two half-holidays weekly; a fortnight at Christmas, Easter, and Pentecost; and a whole month at the harvest-time.

More detailed Statement.

A still more detailed statement of the work of the seven classes is to be obtained by reading what we have already said of the Text-books in Part III., and by what follows :—

I. *The Vestibulary Class.*—On the four walls of the class-room should be painted the Latin characters, models of the regular declensions and conjugations, and brief moral precepts.

By means of a thorough study of the *Vestibulum* in the way already laid down, the class will acquire a knowledge of things in an elementary and yet fundamental way, and also of the roots of words,—that is to say, it will be instructed in the foundations of all intelligence ; and in addition to this, it will be instructed in morality in a form suited to boyhood. The rudiments of arithmetic will at this stage be given, a knowledge of weights, measures, and geometrical forms, and music. The teacher will take advantage of the *words* learned to add to the *knowledge* of the pupils.

II. *The Janual Class.*—On one wall should be painted illustrations of the most important natural objects mentioned in the text of the *Janua*, and opposite these the more important artificial objects should be drawn. The remaining two walls should be occupied with grammatical warnings, having reference to the peculiarities of the pupil's mother-tongue.

In religion the Catechism should at this stage be thoroughly learned.

The knowledge of things and words and grammatical construction is to be obtained from the *Janua.*

Addition and Subtraction in Arithmetic ; the plane figures in Geometry, and Music, are to be taught.

The Composition exercises will consist of the construction of clauses and sentences on the foundation of the words and rules of the *Janua.*

III. *The Atrial Class.*—The walls should be painted over with emblems, and with a selection of warnings regarding the elegancies of writing and speech.

In religion the work of this class will be to read an epitome of Scripture (in Scripture words), and to learn by heart a collection of psalms, hymns, and prayers. The pupils will make acquaintance also with those narratives which are likely to generate virtue and piety.

In addition to the proper study of the Atrial Textbook, Division and Multiplication in arithmetic, and instruction in solid figures, should be given. Music will be continued and select verses from the Latin poets read. Exercises in style on the basis of the Atrium will be given.

At this stage the *Schola Ludus* is to be introduced. This, as I have elsewhere explained, was simply the *Janua* thrown into dramatic form in accordance with the author's conviction that all the work of the Latin school might take a gamesome form.

1V. *The Philosophical Class.*—On the walls of this class-room things are to be represented connected with arithmetic, geometry, statics, anatomy.

In religious instruction, hymns and forms of morning and evening prayer, and of prayers before and after meals and studies, and a life of Christ harmonised from the four Gospels, are to be read.

The class-book will be the first Palace of Wisdom, in which there will be a survey and explanation of all objects of nature written in a style higher and more ornate than the style of the previous books.

The Rule of Three in Arithmetic, Geometry, Trigonometry, and the elements of Statics, are to be taught; also Instrumental Music, and Natural History made up out of Ælian and Pliny.

As to style, which ought now to be on the model of classical authors : this will be suspended so as to admit of the last of the afternoon hours being devoted to Greek, the object being to give sufficient Greek to enable the boys, when they reach the subsequent classes, to read the New Testament in the original.

V. *The Logical Class.*—The walls of the class-room should be painted over with a selection of Rules of Logic and ingenious emblems representing emanations of mind.[1] The religious instruction shall include the

---

[1] Whatever this may mean.

study of a collection of hymns and prayers and a manual of the whole Bible, to be called the *Gate of the Sanctuary*, in which the substance of the sacred writings, as much as possible in the words of Holy. Writ itself, will be given : also a chapter of the Greek New Testament should be read daily.

The afternoon hours should be devoted to Arithmetic, Geometry, Astronomy, Geography, and the elements of Optics, along with the History of Mechanical Inventions.

The class-book belonging to this stage will contain a free treatment of various arts and a strict scientific treatment of one, so as to bring into view the characteristics of exact scientific truth as distinguished from opinion.

Exercises in style should be given at this stage on the model of the historians—Cæsar, Curtius, Nepos, and Justin. The study of Greek is to be carried on by those only who desire to prosecute that language specially : these should read Greek orators, such as Isocrates, and also the *Moralia* of Plutarch.

VI. *The Political Class.*—The pictures on the class wall should represent the significance of order and connection; *e.g.* there should be pictures of the human body wanting certain limbs, others having a superabundance of limbs, and one complete and well-formed.

In religion the full text of Scripture will be studied.

The class-book (the third book of Universal Wisdom) will treat of human society.

Besides the applications of Arithmetic (*ex arithmeticis*

Logistica?), applications of Geometry to Architecture, the theory of the planets, and the doctrine of eclipses, will be taught: compendiums of the geography of the world will also be made.

For the sake of style, Sallust and Cicero, Virgil and Horace, will be read. The pupils will now discuss questions in Latin prescribed beforehand, and be encouraged to use greater freedom in their Latin style. Verse-making yields no fruit worthy of the labour, but should not be prohibited in the case of·those who have a disposition that way.

Those desirous of continuing their Greek studies should read Thucydides and the poets.

VII. *The Theological Class.*—Scriptural emblems, shadowing forth the mysteries of Theology, should adorn three sides of the class-room, and one should be devoted to tables of the Hebrew Grammar and to select Hebrew sayings.

The class-book, the concluding Palace of Wisdom, should explain the intercourse of souls with God, etc. Mathematics should consist of a study of sacred architecture ; *e.g.* the construction of the Mosaic Tabernacle, the Temple of Solomon, etc. The history taught should be universal history, with special reference to the history of the Church and the order of Divine Providence. The exercises in style should be in sacred subjects; and, in addition to these various studies, Hebrew should be acquired.

In the treatise *De Latinae linguae studio perfecté insti-*

tuendo Dissertatio Didactica, published in 1637, he assumes that the upper classes read selections from classical authors, which he proposes to arrange in four books—Epistolary, Historical, Oratorical, and Poetical,[1] and that the relative Lexicon, either in Latin-vernacular or vernacular-Latin, should be a Lexicon of phrases, idioms, and varieties of expression; *e.g.* under the word *Dubito* would come the following words and expressions, Haereo, hesito. Ambigo. Fluctuo, Incertus sum quid agam. Incertum mihi est. In ancipiti sum; and so forth.

Looking to the exercises in style prescribed in Comenius's latest edition of his educational views, as given above, I think we must assume that the selections from classical authors were to be read along with the special class-book of the year; if not by all, at least by all who could overtake them: and this, notwithstanding the fact that extracts from classical authors would doubtless be introduced into the class-books, in so far as relevant to their subject-matter.

Thus in the space of seven years, beginning at twelve years of age, the human being will be formed to a whole and complete humanity in respect of Things, Tongues, Morality, and Piety; he will be able to judge of all things, and in no important thing to err; and, fortified with the elements of universal knowledge, he may now be allowed to study all books, human and divine, and enter on the business of life.

---

[1] *Palatium Epistolicum,* with a hundred epistles; *Palatium Historicum, P. Oratorium, P. Poeticum.*

CONCLUSION.

As Comenius increased in years the religious element in his educational theories assumed more and more prominence. But he never lost sight of his leading principles. The object of all education was to train children to be sons of God, but the way to this was through knowledge, and knowledge was through method. His disposition to see fanciful parallels in nature increased, and Scripture more and more seemed to him to confirm his teachings. A mystical tendency was manifested in his final works written in Amsterdam between 1654-57, especially in his final educational utterance written in Amsterdam, and entitled,—

' *The Idea of Didactic out of the Eternal Arcana.*

'The Son can do nothing of himself, save what he seeth the Father do; for what things soever he doeth, these also doeth the Son likewise. The Father loveth the Son, and sheweth him all things.'—*John* v. 19.

From this flow the following propositions (since the 'invisible things of God from the creation of the world are clearly seen, being understood by the things that are made,' Rom. i. 20) :—

1. That schools ought to be a kind of imitation of heaven.

2. That the intercourse of teachers with taught ought to be like that of fathers with sons.

3. That sons are able to know and do nothing of themselves.

4. Whatever therefore they ought to know or to do (both here and for eternity),—all should be first shown to them.

5. That the said showing beforehand devolves on fathers, that is, on teachers.

6. And this, not by presenting examples alien to the matter in hand, but proper to it, so that things that have to be done may be taught by doing them.

7. That the imitation of all things be exacted in a paternal spirit.

8. And that it be exacted so that sons may do all things in like manner as the example.

On the other hand the eternal idea is departed from whenever—

1. All things are done in any sort of fashion, regard being had to no type, much less the best.

2. The intercourse of teachers with pupils is nothing else save that of hirelings with sheep—for the sake of the fat and the wool.

3. The pupils are left to themselves, and are required to do what they have not yet been taught to do, as if they were able of themselves to know what a teacher knows.

4. And are not taught all things necessary for this life and the next, but only scraps.

5. And the teacher does not teach all things himself, but commits them to another, or presents to the pupil a dumb teacher—a book.

6. And what he teaches he does not teach by,

examples, but by precepts, and, when the pupil does not do what he is ordered, by blows.

7. Or, when he *does* give examples, gives what are alien to the matter in hand, and does not show how they are to be rightly imitated.

8. Or, if he show examples, does not insist on the imitation of them by much and constant practice.

9. And does not exact that imitation in such a way as to make of every pupil a master capable of doing things equal to what has been pointed out to him as models.

This is the sum of all that I wish to have done by those who undertake to rear little sons of God. I have no more to say. And you, gentlemen, with your schools and all the youth of your city[1] dedicated to Christ, I commend to the grace of God, and myself to your favour; signing these my last utterances on Education on the day of the conversion of Paul, on which may the hearts of us all turn to the Lord saying, as Saul said, ' Lord, what wilt thou have me to do ?'

And now, O Jesus Christ, Eternal Wisdom, who rejoicest in the habitable parts of the earth, and whose delight is among the sons of men, who wast well pleased, when dwelling with us in the flesh, to converse with little ones and to think them worthy of Thy embraces as being heirs of the Kingdom of Heaven, count worthy of Thy favour now those who do not disdain to serve Thy little ones ; so that by means of them Thy Blessed Kingdom, here of Grace, there of Glory, may receive a goodly increase, worthy of Thee, the King of the Eternal World. Amen. Amen. Amen.

[1] Amsterdam.

BRIEF CRITICAL SURVEY.

THE object of this volume is to present Comenius himself to the English reader—not Comenius as I may understand him. The latter would have been a comparatively easy task; the task which I have undertaken has been a laborious one. The historical position of Comenius, and his relation to his predecessors, have been brought into view in the Introduction, and his educational aims and labours have been fully set forth in the sketch of his life. The actual work he did is also fully and succinctly set before the reader. We have now only to survey critically the leading characteristics of his system.

The Realism of the Humanists had failed to produce the results they had anticipated. It was in England and Scotland, rather than on the continent of Europe, that the genuine Humanistic spirit was most active in schools. But not for long. Schools and schoolmasters fell back under the dominion of words, abstract propositions, and barren logicalities. This was inevitable. The preoccupation of men's minds with theological and political strife caused the true significance of the educational revival to fall out of sight. The indispensable condition, moreover, of the continuance of the methods of Trotzendorf, and Sturm, and Ascham, was a school of Teachers, and a tradition of Method. There was neither the one nor the other.

Comenius's inspiring motive, like that of all leading educationalists, was social regeneration. He believed that this could be accomplished through the school. He lived under the hallucination that by a proper arrangement of the subject-matter of instruction, and by a sound method, a certain community of thought and interests would be established among the young, which would result in social harmony and political settlement. He believed that men could be manufactured. Had we Chinese to deal with, the dream of educational enthusiasts might possibly be realised; but its realisation would be a misfortune. We have, happily, not Chinese to deal with, but the strong and vigorous European races, full of character and individuality,— the loss of which would be the loss of manhood. Variety, inequality, and strife seem to be essential to the true life of the higher races.

Humanism, which had practically failed in the school, had, apart from this fact, no attractions for Comenius, and still less had the worldly wisdom of Montaigne. He was a leading Protestant theologian,—the pastor and bishop of a small but earnest and devoted sect,—and it was as such that he wrote on Education. The best results of Humanism could, after all, be only culture, and this not necessarily accompanied by moral earnestness or personal piety: on the contrary, probably dissociated from these, and leaning rather to scepticism and intellectual self-indulgence. At the same time, it must be noted that he never fairly faced the Humanistic question; he rather gave it the cold shoulder from the first. His whole nature pointed in another direction. When he has to speak of the great instruments of Humanistic education,—the ancient classical writers,—he exhibits great distrust of them, and if he does not banish them from the school altogether, it is simply because the higher instruction in the Latin and Greek tongues is seen to be impossible without them. Even in the Universities, as his Pansophic scheme shows, he would have had Plato and Aristotle taught chiefly by means of analyses and epitomes. It might be urged in opposition to this view of the anti-Humanism of Comenius, that he contemplated the acquisition of a good style in Latin in the higher stages of instruction: true, but in so far as he did so, it was merely with a practical aim,—the more effective and, if need be, oratorical enforcement of moral and religious truth. The beauties and subtleties of artistic expression had little charm for him, nor did he set much store by the graces. The most conspicuous illustration of the absence of all idea of Art in Comenius is to be found in his school drama. The unprofitable dreariness of that production would make a reader sick were he not relieved by a feeling of its absurdity.

The educational spirit of the Reformers, the conviction that all—even the humblest—must be taught to *know* God, and Jesus Christ whom He has sent, was inherited by Comenius in its completeness. In this way, and in this way only, could the ills of Europe be remedied, and the progress of humanity assured. While, therefore, he sums up the educational aim under the threefold heads of Knowledge, Virtue, and Piety or Godliness, he in truth has mainly in view the last two. Knowledge is of value only in so far as it forms the only sound basis, in the eyes of a Protestant theologian, of virtue and godliness. We have to train for a hereafter.

In virtue and godliness Comenius did not propose to teach anything save what the Reformed religion taught. His characteristic merits in this department of instruction were these :—

1. Morality and godliness were to be taught from the first. Parents and teachers were to begin to train at the beginning of the child's conscious life.

2. Parents and teachers were to give milk to babes, and reserve the stronger meat for the adolescent and adult mind. They were to be content to proceed gradually, step by step.

3. The method of procedure was not only to be adapted to the growing mind, but the mode of enforcement was to be mild, and the manner of it kind and patient.

Had Comenius done nothing more but put forth and press home these truths he would have deserved our gratitude as an educationalist.

But he did more than this. He related virtue and godliness to *Knowledge*. By knowledge Comenius meant knowledge of nature and of man's relation to nature. It is this important characteristic of Comenius's educational system that reveals the direct influence of Bacon and his school. To the great Verulam he pays reverence for what he owed him, but he owed him even more than he knew.

In this field of *Knowledge*, the leading characteristic of the educational system of Comenius is his Realism. We have pointed out,[1] in contradiction of the assumptions of the modern sensationalist school, that the Humanists were in truth Realists, and it may be safely said that there can be no question among competent judges as to the Realism which ought to characterise all rational and sound instruction. The question rather is as to the field in which the Real is to be sought— in the mind of man, or in external nature. As the former may be called Humanistic-Realism, so the latter may be called Sense or Naturalistic-Realism. Of the latter, Comenius is the true founder, although his indebtedness to Ratich was great. Mere acquisition of the ordered facts of Nature, and man's relation to them, was with him the great aim—if not the sole aim— of all purely intellectual instruction. And here there necessarily entered the governing idea, encyclopædism, or pansophism. Let *all* the arts and sciences, he said, be taught in their elements in all schools, and more fully at each successive stage of the pupil's progress. It is by *knowledge* that we are what we are, and the necessary conclusion from this must be, ' let all things be taught to all.'

It is at this point that many will part company with Comenius. The mind stored with facts, even if these be ordered facts, will not necessarily be much raised in

[1] *See* Introduction.

the scale of humanity as an Intelligence. The natural
powers may be simply overweighted by the process,
and the natural channels of spontaneous Reason choked.
In education, while our main business is to promote
the growth of moral purpose and of a strong sense
of duty, we have to support these by the discipline
of intelligence, and by training to power of work rather
than by information. On the other hand, only those
who are ignorant of the history and the recognised
results of education will wholly abjure Realism in the
Comenian sense; but it has to be assigned its own
place, and nothing more than this, in the education
of a human being. The sum of the matter seems to
be this, that while a due place in all education is to
be assigned to sense-realistic studies, especially in the
earlier years of family and school life, the Humanistic
agencies must always remain the most potent in the
making of a man.

Comenius and his followers, again, confound knowledge with wisdom. He affirms that 'all authors are
to be banished from school except those that give a
knowledge of useful things.' Wisdom is certainly not
to be opposed to knowledge, but it depends more on
a man's power of discrimination, combination, and
imagination, than on the extent of his mental store of
facts. Were it not so, our whole secondary education,
and all the purely disciplinal part of our University
instruction, would be very far astray. If the ancient
tongues are to be learned simply with a view to the
sum of knowledge they contain, it would be absurd to

waste the time of our youth over them. It would be
better to impose on our Universities the duty of furnishing guaranteed translations for the use of the public.
We shall not, however, involve ourselves in controversy
here, as our object is merely to point out, generally,
the strong and weak points of our author.

Next in importance to pansophy or encyclopædism,
and closely connected with it, is the principle that a
knowledge of words and of things should go hand in hand.
Words are to be learned through things. Properly
interpreted, and under due limitations, this principle
will, we presume, be now generally accepted. We say,
under due limitations, because it is manifest that the
converse proposition, that 'things are learned through
words,' is easily capable of proof, and is indeed, in our
opinion, the stronghold of Humanistic teaching in its
earlier or school stages.

It is in the department of *Method*, however, that we
recognise the chief contribution of Comenius to education. The mere attempt to systematise was a great
advance. In seeking, however, for foundations on which
to erect a coherent system, he had to content himself
with first principles which were vague and unscientific.

Modern Psychology was in its infancy, and Comenius
had little more than the generalisations of Plato and
Aristotle, and those not strictly investigated by him, for
his guide. In training to virtue, moral truth and the
various moralities were assumed as if they emerged
full-blown in the consciousness of man. In training to

godliness, again, Christian dogma was ready to his hand. In the department of knowledge, that is to say, knowledge of the outer world, Comenius rested his method on the scholastic maxim, *Nihil est in intellectu quod non prius fuerit in sensu.* This maxim he enriched with the Baconian induction, comprehended by him however only in a general way. It was chiefly, however, the imagined harmony of physical and mental processes that yielded his method. He believed that the processes of the growth of external things had a close resemblance to the growth of mind. Had he lived in these days he would doubtless have endeavoured to work out the details of his method on a purely psychological basis; but in the then state of psychology he had to find another thread through the labyrinth. The mode of demonstration which he adopted was thus, as he himself called it, the Syncretic or Analogical. Whatever may be said of the harmony that exists between the growth of nature and of mind, there can be no doubt that the observation of the former is capable of suggesting, if it does not furnish, many of the rules of educational method.

From the simple to the complex, from the particular to the general, the concrete before the abstract, and all, step by step, and even by insensible degrees,—these were among his leading principles of method. But the most important of all his principles was derived from the scholastic maxim quoted above. As all is from sense, let the thing to be known be itself presented to the senses, and let every sense be engaged in the perception of it. When it is impossible, from the nature of the case, to present the object itself, place a vivid picture of it before the pupil. The mere enumeration of these few principles, even if we drop out of view all his other contributions to method and school-management, will satisfy any man familiar with all the more recent treatises on Education, that Comenius, even after giving his precursors their due, is to be regarded as the true founder of modern Method, and that he anticipates Pestalozzi and all of the same school.

When we come to consider Comenius's method as specially applied to language, we recognise its general truth, and the teachers of Europe and America will now be prepared to pay it the homage of theoretical approval at least. To admire, however, his own attempt at working out his linguistic method is impossible, unless we first accept his encyclopædism. The very faults with which he charged the school practices of the time are simply repeated by himself in a new form. The boy's mind is overloaded with a mass of words— the names and qualities of everything in heaven, on the earth, and under the earth. It was impossible that all these things, or even pictures of them, could be presented to sense, and hence his books must have inflicted a heavy burden on the merely verbal memory of boys. We want children to grow into knowledge, not to swallow numberless facts made up into boluses. Again, the amount that was to be acquired within a given time was beyond the youthful capacity. Any teacher will satisfy himself of this who will simply count the words and sentences in the *Janua* and *Orbis*, and then try to distribute these over the school-time allowed by Comenius. Like all reformers, Comenius was over-sanguine. I do not overlook the fact that command over the Latin tongue as a vehicle of expression was the prime necessity of the time for all who meant to devote themselves to professions and to learning, and that Comenius had this justification for introducing a mass of vocables now wholly useless to the student of Latin. But even for his own time, Comenius, under the influence of his encyclopædic passion, overdid his task. His real merits in language-teaching lie in the introduction of the principle of graduated reading-books, in the simplification of Latin grammar, in his founding instruction in foreign tongues on the vernacular, and in his insisting on method in instruction. But these were great merits, too soon forgotten by the dull race of schoolmasters, if, indeed, they were ever fully recognised by them till quite recent times.

Finally, Comenius's views as to the inner organisation of a school were original, and have proved themselves in all essential respects correct.

The same may be said of his scheme for the organisation of a State-system—a scheme which is substantially, *mutatis mutandis*, at this moment embodied in the highly-developed system of Germany.

When we consider, then, that Comenius first formally and fully developed educational method, that he introduced important reforms into the teaching of languages, that he introduced into schools the study of Nature, that he advocated with intelligence, and not on purely sentimental grounds, a milder discipline, we are justified in assigning to him a high, if not the highest, place among modern educational writers. The voluminousness of his treatises, their prolixity, their repetitions, and their defects of style, have all operated to prevent men studying him. The substance of all he has written has been, I believe, faithfully given by me, but it has not been possible to transfer to these pages the fervour, the glow, and the pious aspirations of the good old Bishop.

If any are disposed to regard with impatience the encyclopædic proposals of Comenius, I would have them consider that two great Englishmen, Milton and Locke, shared substantially the same views. And when we compare a youth who has been instructed merely in the bare, bald facts of the outer world, and his relation to them, with a youth who has been left to himself, we rightly conclude that there is a certain educational power even in mere information. And yet the summed-up result, in respect of intelligence and character, in the case of youths of encyclopædic and superficial acquisitions is not satisfactory. On the contrary, it is sadly disappointing when compared with the labour expended by both teacher and taught. On the other hand, we certainly find the supreme educational result—that is to say, wisdom, virtue, and capacity for affairs—to have been attained (as nearly as human imperfection admits of) by a totally different process. We are thus forced to revise our theories. The way whereby nature makes a mind is not so plain as at first appears. If educators could find that secret way, it would doubtless be their duty to follow it, cost what it might. It will probably however, be found that while there can be only one true general method in education, the maximum of mental capacity is attainable by different individuals by means of different studies, for the simple reason that the food which can be assimilated by one cannot be assimilated by another. The conclusion to be drawn from this (and I think it a very important one in all education) is that no school-curriculum should be so arranged as to use up all a pupil's brain energy. Time should be left for the indulgence of idiosyncracies even if these run in the direction of apparent idleness and day-dreaming.

In seeking to ascertain our duty as Educators, let us not wilfully exaggerate differences in modes of procedure where there is essential community of aim. All educationalists, of whatsoever school, who have endeavoured seriously to think on the subject on which they write, desire to produce wise, virtuous, religious and capable men with bodies fitted to be an apt vehicle of Spirit. 'Culture,' it is true, is the deity which some worship, but it is difficult to say what culture is, and until we have settled this, we may leave it out of account. This we can safely affirm, that self culture is possible only by the culture of that which is not self. Were any man to propose himself to himself as the object of his self-discipline, he would emerge from the educational laboratory

a narrow-souled, insufferable prig.   Culture from another
point of view leads only to that most detestable of all
civilized products—an "elegant mind."   Let us drop
culture, then, and confine ourselves to the common
ground of wisdom, virtue and religion, and if it be by
any means possible among us northern nations, let us
add the grace of courtesy which the Greeks called
εὐκοσμία.   All agree so far, and the question at issue
these three hundred years, and still unsettled, is by what
processes can this supreme end be best attained?   By
moral instruction and training, all alike answer ; but by
what further instruments?   By the study of man and of
human life and thought, as these are embodied for us
in language and literature, or by the study of external
nature and our relations to it ?   We do not propose
here to attempt to answer the question, but in the
debate between Humanists and Sense-Realists there is a
growing consensus visible.   For all thinkers will, I think,
now admit that up to the age of puberty at least, subjects
which appeal to the senses and connect a boy with
external nature ought to take precedence of all others
except the vernacular language and arithmetic, and that
after that age the instruction should be more formal and
severe and based principally on Language, Literature and
Mathematics.   Thus far, the incontestable facts of psychology and physiology settle the wordy war on scientific
grounds.   The same facts point to the conclusion that
even encyclopædism, in a restricted sense, has its place,
at least in the earlier stages of education.

NOTE ON p. 40.

Hartlib also was the author of a scheme for an Agricultural College contained in his "Propositions for the erecting of a College of Husbandry learning" 1651, and it was to him that Sir W. Petty wrote in 1647 a letter containing a scheme for a great technical College where "all apprentices might learn the theory of their trades before they are bound to a Master" &c.*

* Quoted by Mr Browning in his Educational Theories.

INDEX.

CAMBRIDGE: PRINTED BY C. J. CLAY, M.A. & SONS, AT THE UNIVERSITY PRESS.

SOME PUBLICATIONS OF THE

CAMBRIDGE UNIVERSITY PRESS.

THE PITT PRESS SERIES.

I. GREEK.

Aristophanes. Aves—Plutus—Ranæ. By W. C. GREEN, M.A., late Assistant Master at Rugby School. 3s. 6d. each.

Aristotle. Outlines of the Philosophy of. Compiled by EDWIN WALLACE, M.A., LL.D. Third Edition, Enlarged. 4s. 6d.

Euripides. Heracleidæ. With Introduction and Critical Notes. By E. A. BECK, M.A., Fellow of Trinity Hall. 3s. 6d.

Euripides. Hercules Furens. With Introduction, Notes and Analysis. By A. GRAY, M.A., and J. T. HUTCHINSON, M.A. New Ed. 2s.

Herodotus, Book VIII., Chaps. 1—90. Edited with Notes and Introduction. By E. S. SHUCKBURGH, M.A. 3s. 6d.

—— **Book IX., Chaps. 1—89.** By the same Editor. 3s. 6d.

Homer. Odyssey, Book IX. With Introduction, Notes and Appendices by G. M. EDWARDS, M.A. 2s. 6d.

Luciani Somnium Charon Piscator et De Luctu. By W. E. HEITLAND, M.A., Fellow of St John's College, Cambridge. 3s. 6d.

Platonis Apologia Socratis. With Introduction, Notes and Appendices. By J. ADAM, M.A. 3s. 6d.

—— **Crito.** With Introduction, Notes and Appendix. By the same Editor. 2s. 6d.

Plutarch. Lives of the Gracchi. With Introduction, Notes and Lexicon by Rev. H. A. HOLDEN, M.A., LL.D. 6s.

—— **Life of Nicias.** With Introduction and Notes by the same Editor. 5s.

—— **Life of Sulla.** With Introduction, Notes, and Lexicon. By the same Editor. 6s.

Sophocles. Oedipus Tyrannus. School Edition, with Introduction and Commentary by R. C. JEBB, Litt.D., LL.D. 4s. 6d.

Xenophon. Agesilaus. By H. HAILSTONE, M.A., late Scholar of Peterhouse, Cambridge. 2s. 6d.

Xenophon. Anabasis. With Introduction, Map and English Notes, by A. PRETOR, M.A. Two vols. 7s. 6d.

—— **Books I. III. IV. and V.** By the same. 2s. each.

—— **Books II. VI. and VII.** By the same. 2s. 6d. each.

Xenophon. Cyropaedeia. Books I. II. With Introduction and Notes by Rev. H. A. HOLDEN, M.A., LL.D. 2 vols. 6s.

—— —— **Books III. IV. and V.** By the same Editor. 5s.

London: Cambridge Warehouse, Ave Maria Lane.

10/10/88

II. LATIN.

Beda's Ecclesiastical History, Books III., IV. Edited with a life, Notes, Glossary, Onomasticon and Index, by J. E. B. MAYOR, M.A., and J. R. LUMBY, D.D. Revised Edition. 7s. 6d.

—— **Books I. II.** By the same Editors.   [*In the Press.*

Caesar. De Bello Gallico, Comment. I. With Maps and Notes by A. G. PESKETT, M.A., Fellow of Magdalene College, Cambridge. 1s. 6d.

—— **Comment. I. II. III.** 3s.

—— **Comment. IV. V., and Comment. VII.** 2s. each.

—— **Comment. VI. and Comment. VIII.** 1s. 6d. each.

Cicero. De Amicitia. Edited by J. S. REID, Litt.D., Fellow of Gonville and Caius College. Revised Edition. 3s. 6d.

Cicero. De Senectute. By the same Editor. 3s. 6d.

Cicero. In Gaium Verrem Actio Prima. With Notes, by H. COWIE, M.A. 1s. 6d.

Cicero. In Q. Caecilium Divinatio et in C. Verrem Actio. With Notes by W. E. HEITLAND, M.A., and H. COWIE, M.A. 3s.

Cicero. Philippica Secunda. With Introduction and Notes by A. G. PESKETT, M.A. 3s. 6d.

Cicero. Oratio pro Archia Poeta. By J. S. REID, Litt.D. Revised Edition. 2s.

Cicero. Pro L. Cornelio Balbo Oratio. By the same. 1s. 6d.

Cicero. Oratio pro Tito Annio Milone, with English Notes, &c., by JOHN SMYTH PURTON, B.D. 2s. 6d.

Cicero. Oratio pro L. Murena, with English Introduction and Notes. By W. E. HEITLAND, M.A. 3s.

Cicero. Pro Cn. Plancio Oratio, by H. A. HOLDEN, LL.D. Second Edition. 4s. 6d.

—— **Pro P. Cornelio Sulla Oratio.** By J. S. REID, Litt.D. 3s. 6d.

Cicero. Somnium Scipionis. With Introduction and Notes. Edited by W. D. PEARMAN, M.A. 2s.

Horace. Epistles, Book I. With Notes and Introduction by E. S. SHUCKBURGH, M.A., late Fellow of Emmanuel College. 2s. 6d.

Livy. Book XXI. With Notes, Introduction and Maps. By . M. S. DIMSDALE, M.A., Fellow of King's College. 3s. 6d.

Lucan. Pharsaliae Liber Primus, with English Introduction and Notes by W. E. HEITLAND, M.A., and C. E. HASKINS, M.A. 1s. 6d.

Ovidii Nasonis Fastorum Liber VI. With Notes by A. SIDGWICK, M.A., Tutor of Corpus Christi College, Oxford. 1s. 6d.

Quintus Curtius. A Portion of the History (Alexander in India). By W. E. HEITLAND, M.A., and T. E. RAVEN, B.A. With Two Maps. 3s. 6d.

Vergili Maronis Aeneidos Libri I.—XII. Edited with Notes by A. SIDGWICK, M.A. 1s. 6d. each.

—— **Bucolica.** With Introduction and Notes by the same Editor. 1s. 6d.

—— **Georgicon Libri I. II.** By the same Editor. 2s.

—— —— **Libri III. IV.** By the same Editor. 2s.

III. FRENCH.

Corneille. La Suite du Menteur. A Comedy in Five Acts. With Notes Philological and Historical, by the late G. MASSON, B.A. 2s.

De Bonnechose. Lazare Hoche. With three Maps, Introduction and Commentary, by C. COLBECK, M.A. 2s.

D'Harleville. Le Vieux Célibataire. A Comedy, Grammatical and Historical Notes, by G. MASSON, B.A. 2s.

De Lamartine. Jeanne D'Arc. Edited with a Map and Notes Historical and Philological, and a Vocabulary, by Rev. A. C. CLAPIN, M.A., St John's College, Cambridge. 2s.

De Vigny. La Canne de Jonc. Edited with Notes by Rev. H. A. BULL, M.A., late Master at Wellington College. 2s.

Erckmann-Chatrian. La Guerre. With Map, Introduction and Commentary by Rev. A. C. CLAPIN, M.A. 3s.

La Baronne de Staël-Holstein. Le Directoire. (Considérations sur la Révolution Française. Troisième et quatrième parties.) Revised and enlarged. With Notes by G. MASSON, B.A. and G. W. PROTHERO, M.A. 2s.

—— **Dix Années d'Exil. Livre II. Chapitres 1—8.** By the same Editors. New Edition, enlarged. 2s.

Lemercier. Fredegonde et Brunehaut. A Tragedy in Five Acts. By GUSTAVE MASSON, B.A. 2s.

Molière. Le Bourgeois Gentilhomme, Comédie-Ballet en Cinq Actes. (1670.) By Rev. A. C. CLAPIN, M.A. 1s. 6d.

—— **L'Ecole des Femmes.** With Introduction and Notes by G. SAINTSBURY, M.A. 2s. 6d.

Piron. La Métromanie. A Comedy, with Notes, by G. MASSON, B.A. 2s.

Sainte-Beuve. M. Daru (Causeries du Lundi, Vol. IX.) By G. MASSON, B.A. 2s.

Saintine. Picciola. With Introduction, Notes and Map. By Rev. A. C. CLAPIN, M.A. 2s.

Scribe and Legouvé. Bataille de Dames. Edited by Rev. H. A. BULL, M.A. 2s.

Scribe. Le Verre d'Eau. A Comedy; with Memoir, Grammatical and Historical Notes. Edited by C. COLBECK, M.A. 2s.

Sedaine. Le Philosophe sans le savoir. Edited with Notes by Rev. H. A. BULL, M.A., late Master at Wellington College. 2s.

Thierry. Lettres sur l'histoire de France (XIII.—XXIV). By G. MASSON, B.A. and G. W. PROTHERO, M.A. 2s. 6d.

——— **Récits des Temps Mérovingiens I—III.** Edited by GUSTAVE MASSON, B.A. Univ. Gallic., and A. R. ROPES, M.A. With Map. 3s.

Villemain. Lascaris ou Les Grecs du XVe Siècle, Nouvelle Historique. By G. MASSON, B.A. 2s.

Voltaire. Histoire du Siècle de Louis XIV. Chaps. I.— XIII. Edited with Notes by G. MASSON, B.A. and G. W. PROTHERO, M.A. 2s. 6d.

——— **Part II. Chaps. XIV—XXIV.** By the same Editors. With Three Maps. 2s. 6d.

——— **Part III. Chaps. XXV. to end.** By the same Editors. 2s. 6d.

Xavier de Maistre. La Jeune Siberienne. Le Lépreux de la Cité D'Aoste. By G. MASSON, B.A. 2s.

IV. GERMAN.

Ballads on German History. Arranged and annotated by WILHELM WAGNER, Ph.D. 2s.

Benedix. Doctor Wespe. Lustspiel in fünf Aufzügen. Edited with Notes by KARL HERMANN BREUL, M.A. 3s.

Freytag. Der Staat Friedrichs des Grossen. With Notes. By WILHELM WAGNER, Ph.D. 2s.

German Dactylic Poetry. Arranged and annotated by WILHELM WAGNER, Ph.D. 2s.

Goethe's Knabenjahre. (1749—1759.) Arranged and annotated by WILHELM WAGNER, Ph.D. 2s.

——— **Hermann und Dorothea.** By WILHELM WAGNER, Ph.D. Revised edition by J. W. CARTMELL, M.A. 3s. 6d.

Gutzkow. Zopf und Schwert. Lustspiel in fünf Aufzügen. By H. J. WOLSTENHOLME, B.A. (Lond.). 3s. 6d.

Hauff. Das Wirthshaus im Spessart. By A. SCHLOTTMANN, Ph.D. 3s. 6d.

Hauff. Die Karavane. Edited with Notes by A. SCHLOTTMANN, Ph.D. 3s. 6d.

Immermann. Der Oberhof. A tale of Westphalian Life, by WILHELM WAGNER, Ph.D. 3s.

Kohlrausch. Das Jahr 1813. With English Notes by WILHELM WAGNER, Ph.D. 2s.

Lessing and Gellert. Selected Fables. Edited with Notes by KARL HERMANN BREUL, M.A., Lecturer in German at the University of Cambridge. 3s.

Mendelssohn's Letters. Selections from. Edited by JAMES
SIME, M.A. 3*s.*

Raumer. Der erste Kreuzzug (1095—1099). By WILHELM
WAGNER, Ph.D. 3*s.*

Riehl. Culturgeschichtliche Novellen. Edited by H. J.
WOLSTENHOLME, B.A. (Lond.). 4*s.* 6*d.*

Uhland. Ernst, Herzog von Schwaben. With Introduction
and Notes. By the same Editor. 3*s.* 6*d.*

V. ENGLISH.

Ancient Philosophy from Thales to Cicero, A Sketch of. By
JOSEPH B. MAYOR, M.A. 3*s.* 6*d.*

Bacon's History of the Reign of King Henry VII. With
Notes by the Rev. Professor LUMBY, D.D. 3*s.*

Cowley's Essays. With Introduction and Notes, by the Rev.
Professor LUMBY, D.D. 4*s.*

Geography, Elementary Commercial. A Sketch of the Com-
modities and the Countries of the World. By H. R. MILL, Sc.D., F.R.S.E. 1*s.*

More's History of King Richard III. Edited with Notes,
Glossary, Index of Names. By J. RAWSON LUMBY, D.D. 3*s.* 6*d.*

More's Utopia. With Notes, by Rev. Prof. LUMBY, D.D. 3*s.*

The Two Noble Kinsmen, edited with Introduction and Notes,
by the Rev. Professor SKEAT, Litt.D. 3*s.* 6*d.*

VI. EDUCATIONAL SCIENCE.

Comenius, John Amos, Bishop of the Moravians. His Life
and Educational Works, by S. S. LAURIE, A.M., F.R.S.E. New Edition,
revised. 3*s.* 6*d.*

Education, Three Lectures on the Practice of. Delivered
under the direction of the Teachers' Training Syndicate. 2*s.*

Locke on Education. With Introduction and Notes by the
Rev. R. H. QUICK, M.A. 3*s.* 6*d.*

Milton's Tractate on Education. A facsimile reprint from
the Edition of 1673. Edited, with Introduction and Notes, by OSCAR
BROWNING, M.A. 2*s.*

Modern Languages, Lectures on the Teaching of. By C.
COLBECK, M.A. 2*s.*

Teacher, General aims of the, and Form Management. Two
Lectures delivered in the University of Cambridge in the Lent Term, 1883, by
F. W. FARRAR, D.D. and R. B. POOLE, B.D. 1*s.* 6*d.*

Teaching, Theory and Practice of. By the Rev. E. THRING,
M.A., late Head Master of Uppingham School. New Edition. 4*s.* 6*d.*

Other Volumes are in preparation.

London: Cambridge Warehouse, Ave Maria Lane.

The Cambridge Bible for Schools and Colleges.

GENERAL EDITOR: J. J. S. PEROWNE, D.D.,
DEAN OF PETERBOROUGH.

"It is difficult to commend too highly this excellent series."—
Guardian.

"The modesty of the general title of this series has, we believe, led many to misunderstand its character and underrate its value. The books are well suited for study in the upper forms of our best schools, but not the less are they adapted to the wants of all Bible students who are not specialists. We doubt, indeed, whether any of the numerous popular commentaries recently issued in this country will be found more serviceable for general use."—*Academy.*

"Of great value. The whole series of comments for schools is highly esteemed by students capable of forming a judgment. The books are scholarly without being pretentious: information is so given as to be easily understood."—*Sword and Trowel.*

NOW READY. Cloth, Extra Fcap. 8vo.

Book of Joshua. By Rev. G. F. MACLEAR, D.D. With Maps. 2s. 6d.

Book of Judges. By Rev. J. J. LIAS, M.A.. 3s. 6d.

First Book of Samuel. By Rev. Prof. KIRKPATRICK, M.A. With Map. 3s. 6d.

Second Book of Samuel. By Rev. Prof. KIRKPATRICK, M.A. With 2 Maps. 3s. 6d.

First Book of Kings. By Rev. Prof. LUMBY, D.D. With 3 Maps. 3s. 6d.

Second Book of Kings. By Rev. Prof. LUMBY, D.D. With 3 Maps. 3s. 6d.

Book of Job. By Rev. A. B. DAVIDSON, D.D. 5s.

Book of Ecclesiastes. By Very Rev. E. H. PLUMPTRE, D.D. 5s.

Book of Jeremiah. By Rev. A. W. STREANE, M.A. 4s. 6d.

Book of Hosea. By Rev. T. K. CHEYNE, M.A., D.D. 3s.

London: Cambridge Warehouse, Ave Maria Lane.

Books of Obadiah and Jonah. By Arch. PEROWNE. 2s. 6d.

Book of Micah. By Rev. T. K. CHEYNE, M.A., D.D. 1s. 6d.

Books of Haggai and Zechariah. By Arch. PEROWNE. 3s.

Gospel according to St Matthew. By Rev. A. CARR, M.A. With 2 Maps. 2s. 6d.

Gospel according to St Mark. By Rev. G. F. MACLEAR, D.D. With 4 Maps. 2s. 6d.

Gospel according to St Luke. By Archdeacon FARRAR. With 4 Maps. 4s. 6d.

Gospel according to St John. By Rev. A. PLUMMER, M.A., D.D. With 4 Maps. 4s. 6d.

Acts of the Apostles. By Rev. Professor LUMBY, D.D. With 4 Maps. 4s. 6d.

Epistle to the Romans. Rev. H. C. G. MOULE, M.A. 3s. 6d.

First Corinthians. By Rev. J. J. LIAS, M.A. With Map. 2s.

Second Corinthians. By Rev. J. J. LIAS, M.A. With Map. 2s.

Epistle to the Ephesians. By Rev. H. C. G. MOULE, M.A. 2s. 6d.

Epistle to the Hebrews. By Arch. FARRAR, D.D. 3s. 6d.

General Epistle of St James. By Very Rev. E. H. PLUMPTRE, D.D. 1s. 6d.

Epistles of St Peter and St Jude. By Very Rev. E. H. PLUMPTRE, D.D. 2s. 6d.

Epistles of St John. By Rev. A. PLUMMER, M.A., D.D. 3s. 6d.

Preparing.

Book of Genesis. By Very Rev. the Dean of Peterborough.

Books of Exodus, Numbers and Deuteronomy. By Rev. C. D. GINSBURG, LL.D.

Books of Ezra and Nehemiah. By Rev. Prof. RYLE, M.A.

Book of Psalms. By Rev. Prof. KIRKPATRICK, M.A.

Book of Isaiah. By W. ROBERTSON SMITH, M.A.

Book of Ezekiel. By Rev. A. B. DAVIDSON, D.D.

Epistle to the Galatians. By Rev. E. H. PEROWNE, D.D.

Epistles to the Philippians, Colossians and Philemon. By Rev. H. C. G. MOULE, M.A.

Epistles to the Thessalonians. By Rev. W. F. MOULTON, D.D.

Book of Revelation. By Rev. W. H. SIMCOX, M.A.

London: Cambridge Warehouse, Ave Maria Lane.

The Cambridge Greek Testament for Schools and Colleges,

with a Revised Text, based on the most recent critical authorities, and English Notes, prepared under the direction of the General Editor,

J. J. S. PEROWNE, D.D., DEAN OF PETERBOROUGH.

Gospel according to St Matthew. By Rev. A. CARR, M.A.
With 4 Maps. 4s. 6d.

Gospel according to St Mark. By Rev. G. F. MACLEAR, D.D.
With 3 Maps. 4s. 6d.

Gospel according to St Luke. By Archdeacon FARRAR.
With 4 Maps. 6s.

Gospel according to St John. By Rev. A. PLUMMER, M.A.
With 4 Maps. 6s.

Acts of the Apostles. By Rev. Professor LUMBY, D.D.
With 4 Maps. 6s.

First Epistle to the Corinthians. By Rev. J. J. LIAS, M.A. 3s.

Second Epistle to the Corinthians. By Rev. J. J. LIAS, M.A.
[*Preparing.*

Epistle to the Hebrews. By Archdeacon FARRAR, D.D.
[*In the Press.*

Epistle of St James. By Very Rev. E. H. PLUMPTRE, D.D.
[*Preparing.*

Epistles of St John. By Rev. A. PLUMMER, M.A., D.D. 4s.

London: C. J. CLAY AND SONS,
CAMBRIDGE WAREHOUSE, AVE MARIA LANE.
Glasgow: 263, ARGYLE STREET.
Cambridge: DEIGHTON, BELL AND CO.
Leipzig: F. A. BROCKHAUS.

CAMBRIDGE: PRINTED BY C. J. CLAY, M.A. AND SONS, AT THE UNIVERSITY PRESS.

www.ingramcontent.com/pod-product-compliance
Lightning Source LLC
Chambersburg PA
CBHW031429020726
47499CB00005B/1660